Also by David Oppegaard

The Firebug of Balrog County
And the Hills Opened Up
Wormwood, Nevada
The Suicide Collectors

Praise for *The Firebug of Balrog County*

"Oppegaard's book is beautifully written and full of honest characters, but probably its finest virtue is giving an authentic and powerful voice to a young man in pain." —*VOYA*

"Take one angry 18-year-old, sprinkle with zingy narrative, and add a match." —*Kirkus Reviews*

"In this biting coming-of-age . . . Oppegaard doesn't offer an easy solution to Mack's problems, instead opting for a realistic and sensitive resolution that leaves on a hopeful note." —*Booklist*

"A great read." —*School Library Connection*

THE TOWN BUILT ON SORROW

THE TOWN BUILT ON SORROW

DAVID OPPEGAARD

Mendota Heights, Minnesota

First Edition
First Printing, 2017

Book design by Madeline Berger
Cover design by Jake Nordby
Cover images by Unsplash/Pexels; freestocks.org/Pexels; Pixabay/Pexels; Sci-setti Alfio/Shutterstock Images; Ensuper/Shutterstock Images
Interior images by Unsplash/Pexels

Flux, an imprint of North Star Editions, Inc.

Library of Congress Cataloging-in-Publication Data (Pending)
978-1-63583-006-4

Flux
North Star Editions, Inc.
2297 Waters Drive
Mendota Heights, MN 55120
www.fluxnow.com

Printed in the United States of America

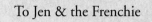

To Jen & the Frenchie

What Should Have Stayed Buried

Olav Helle forgot to check beneath his car and felt a telltale thump as he backed out of his driveway. He'd had his driver's license for only two weeks but he knew a total fuckup when he felt one. He stopped the car immediately and put it in park. He gripped the car's steering wheel so tightly his knuckles turned white and he considered slamming his face into the steering wheel's center—WHAM WHAM WHAM—until his face was so bashed in it would be all but unrecognizable, a pulpy mishmash of skin, blood, and bone.

Instead, Olav turned off the ignition and got out, slamming the driver's side door behind him. He knelt on the gravel driveway and peered beneath his car.

Cooper, the neighbor's plump tabby cat, lay crushed and twitching in the car's shadow.

"Oh, shit."

The cat turned in the direction of his voice. One of its eyes was puffed out bigger than the other and filled with blood. It was fucked.

"Come here, dude."

Olav reached under the car, grabbed the cat, and dragged it into the light. He looked around to see if anyone was watching—you could always see those curtains being pulled back, those blinds parted—but didn't make out any spies. It was a chilly November day in Hawthorn, and his neighborhood was quiet. Olav had driven home from school to eat lunch and nobody else was around, not even the usual gawking old ladies, the ones who always hung around in their front yards in their baggy dresses while they watered shit with a hose. He'd gotten lucky, witness-wise.

The cat twitched and made a sad little mewing sound. Olav grabbed the back of its neck, dug his fingers into its fur, and twisted his wrist sharply, snapping the cat's neck. The cat twitched for a few seconds and then went still as the light in its eyes calcified. Olav stroked the dead cat's fur twice, took a deep breath, and stood up. He knew if his parents found out he'd run over the Rathbones' cat they'd take his driver's license away for a month or longer, and he'd already waited forever to start driving in the first place. It wasn't his fault if Cooper was a sleepy idiot who liked lying beneath cars. This was Darwinism in action.

Okay . . .

Yeah.

He'd hide the evidence as fast as he could and go back to school. The Rathbones would think Cooper had run away, and Olav would avoid getting in trouble. Besides, either way, nothing was bringing this cat back from the dead.

Olav went into his garage, found a shovel, and returned to the crime scene. He scooped up the cat, prayed nobody was watching him, and briskly crossed his backyard and entered the woods behind it. He wove his way through the trees, focusing on the dead cat and doing his best to keep it from sliding off the shovel. The forest was a mishmash of blue spruce, pine, fir, larch, and cedar trees. The air always smelled like sap, and fat pinecones lay strewn on the ground like undetonated grenades. Olav made his way through the trees slowly, listening to the woods. A blue mountain jay flew in front of him and settled on a high branch, giving him the once-over as it turned its arrowhead-shaped crest from side to side. Olav continued on, pushing his way through the trees until he entered the Clearing.

Olav had been going to the Clearing for years. He liked to hang out in it and sit on top of the large boulder at its center. Sometimes he smoked cigarettes if he had any. Sometimes he read comic books. Sometimes he didn't do anything but lie on his back and look up at the clouds through a hole in the forest canopy and listen to the trees rustling around him. The Clearing was peaceful, and he could be alone and untroubled in it, tucked away from his parents and everyone else in town.

Now the Clearing would be a cat graveyard, too. Olav dumped Cooper on the ground and started digging at the base of the big rock—the boulder would make a nice gravestone, fit for a king—and threw shovelfuls of sandy soil to the side. He worked smoothly, breaking through roots and random clumps of clay. He got into the digging and kept going deeper than a cat grave really needed to be until suddenly the shovel hit something hard. He thought it was a rock at first, but as he dug farther he could see an empty white eye socket peering up at him from the bottom of the hole.

"No way."

Olav tossed the shovel aside and knelt at the edge of

the hole. He dug around the eye socket with his hands, and soon the top half of a human skull was revealed, enough skull that Olav could pull it out of the ground like he was harvesting a potato. He scooped dirt out of the skull's eye sockets, brushed off the worms and centipedes clinging to its surface, and held it up to the light.

The skull was yellow with age and missing its jawbone. Olav knocked on its cranium and listened to the hollow sound it made. "That's where your brain used to be," Olav said. "Right under this bone." The skull was missing most of its teeth, but the three that remained still looked long and sharp. Olav ran his finger along the biggest tooth and pictured a huge caveman, jacked with muscles and hairy as a bear, the kind of beast-man who dressed in animal skins and drank the blood of his enemies.

Olav placed the skull on top of the boulder and held its empty stare while he wiped his hands on the front of his jeans. A cold late autumn wind blew through the forest as Olav picked his shovel up off the ground and took a deep breath.

"Just wait a minute," Olav told the skull. "I have to bury something else."

Part One

1

HARPER SPURLING LAY in bed, staring at her laptop's glowing screen in her otherwise darkened bedroom. It was seven a.m., and she'd been up since four, despite her best attempts to go back to sleep. It was as if something had jumped onto Harper's bed and woken her up on purpose—like a hungry cat, or a dog that needed to be let out—but her family didn't have any pets. Not even goldfish. Harper had been deeply asleep, and then something happened, and she was instantly awake.

Wide awake.

But Harper really wanted to sleep. She needed it. She was sixteen and a sophomore in high school, always loaded down with homework, and spring finals were three weeks away. She ran track. She wrote for her school paper. Without sleep, her brain would start to lock up, her eyes would feel scratchy, and she'd turn into a zombie by fourth period.

Footsteps thumped overhead on the basement stairs. Other than an open laundry room and a storage room, Harper had the basement of her house all to herself (as long as you didn't count the spiders and freaky millipedes).

"Harper? Are you awake?"

It was The Mom.

"Yeah?"

"Your dad's making French toast."

"Okay."

Harper kicked off the covers and slid off her bed. She pulled back the heavy blackout curtains and sunlight blasted into the room, revealing piles of clothing stacked on the floor. Harper opened her bedroom door and stood at the foot of the stairs. She could hear her family in the kitchen, and the smell of coffee had increased in piquancy. She started up the stairs, aiming to make as little noise as possible, but The Dad's radar went off as she passed by the kitchen doorway and he popped his head out.

"Hey there, sunshine. Ready for the world's greatest French toast?"

Harper grumbled and waved him away, making a beeline for the hallway and the bathroom at the end of it. The Dad had obviously gotten a lot more sleep than she had.

"Okay. Hurry up before it gets cold!"

Harper closed the bathroom door. After she peed she ran the sink until the water was hot, lathered her hands with soap, and washed her face, imagining that she was a raccoon bathing at the edge of a warm pond. Feeling more refreshed, she left the bathroom and wandered back to the kitchen. "There she is," The Dad said, winking at her. The Mom and The Brothers all looked up. Cameron was ten and Sam was seven—somehow Harper's parents had let a six-year gap slip between having their first and second child.

Harper plunked into her chair and kicked out her long legs. She was five-seven, two inches taller than The Mom, who tried to act as if this didn't bug her.

The Dad set a plate of French toast in front of Harper.

"Thanks, Dad." Harper glanced at The Mom, who was wearing her emerald green house kimono and messing around with a card game on her scratched-up iPad. "Can I have a cup of coffee?"

The Mom looked up.

"Sure. I suppose you're too tall already to be properly stunted."

"Good one," Harper said, getting up and pouring coffee into her old Hello Kitty mug. The half-and-half was sitting out on the counter, probably warm already, but she added a splash to the mug anyway. The Dad stood beside her, stabbing the bits of syrup-soaked French toast on his plate.

"Man, this was good, but I need to get moving," he said to nobody in particular. He put his plate in the sink, kissed The Mom on the top of her head, and left the kitchen, his bathrobe flapping at his heels. This was a typically random The Dad exit.

Harper sat back down at the table. She sipped her coffee and winced—she'd forgotten to add sugar. Harper glanced at her mother, decided that getting up to add sugar would be a kind of defeat, like something a little kid would do, and took another drink before setting the mug down and picking up her fork. The French toast was covered in powdered sugar, anyway. She broke off a piece with her fork and chewed it dry.

"You forgot syrup," Sam said, eyeing her plate. "Don't you want the syrup?"

Harper broke off another piece of French toast and ate

it. Sam grabbed the syrup and set it in front of her plate, his bulbous eyes frog-like behind his thick glasses.

"There."

"Maybe I don't want any syrup," Harper said, pointing at her brother with her fork. "Did you ever think of that?"

"But syrup makes everything better."

"All right," The Mom said, pushing her iPad away and sitting back in her chair. "Everyone just eat your food."

"I'm done," Cameron said, standing up so fast his chair almost fell over.

"Me, too," Sam said, setting his fork on his plate. "I'm full."

"Okay," The Mom said, eyeing their plates. "Put your dishes in the dishwasher and get ready for school."

The Brothers put their plates in the dishwasher while making as big a racket as possible and left the kitchen. Harper uncapped the bottle of syrup and poured it over her French toast as the front door slammed shut. The Mom smiled and drummed the table with her fingers.

"So what's on the high school docket today?"

Harper chewed her food and considered the question. She knew she'd need to come up with one stupid fact or The Mom would drag out the conversation forever. She liked to torture Harper with questions.

"We're talking about Hawthorn in history class."

"Oh, yeah? That's great. You can talk about Daniel Spurling."

"What was he again? A blacksmith?"

"He owned a sawmill. He was a lumberman."

"And he helped start Hawthorn?"

"That's right. He was one of the original founders. He rolled out here with a wagon and his whole family. He was a real pioneer. He's your great-great-great-great grandfather, I think. Or is it five greats?"

Harper took another sip of the not-sweetened coffee and gazed out the kitchen window. The houses across the street all seemed too large, as if they'd started to swell.

"I'm going to stop and visit Grandma before school."

"Good," The Mom said. "She'll like that."

Harper's grandmother lived in Burbling Brook, an assisted-living home on the southern outskirts of town. The home offered a sweeping view of the mountains to the south and had an actual burbling brook running through its backyard. Like everyone else who'd lived in Hawthorn their entire lives, Harper had become so familiar with the Clawhook Mountains that they'd long ago become nothing more than visual white noise to her, worth noting only when the setting sun turned their snowcapped peaks pink, or when heavy weather hung around them, zapping them with lightning.

To old people, however, the mountains were like freaking catnip. The rocking chairs on the home's outdoor promenade were often occupied by residents chewing the fat and smoking pipes, even in winter when they had to cocoon themselves in heavy blankets. They claimed the fresh air was good for them and that looking at the mountains made them feel refreshed and added an extra year or two to their lives.

Harper parked in Burbling Brook's parking lot and approached its main entrance. Though it was only eight a.m., the south porch was packed with bundled-up oldsters. Harper searched the crowd of faces for her grandmother, didn't find her, and headed inside as the groggy crowd watched her pass without comment.

The usual scents of orange antiseptic spray, floor wax, and potpourri with a vague hint of shit lying beneath them greeted Harper as she went inside. She said hello to the nurse at the front desk and continued down the hall to her grandmother's room. She found her still lying in bed, working a crossword puzzle book with her bare, blue-veined feet poking up from beneath her blanket. At eighty years old, Grandma Spurling was small and rail-thin with gray eyes that still shone brightly through her thick trifocal glasses. Her hair, originally blond, had turned a soft, fluffy white and sat atop her head like a wig made out of lamb's wool.

"You're too thin," her grandmother said, clipping her pen to the puzzle book and setting it aside.

"Hi, Grandma."

Harper leaned over and hugged the old woman cautiously, not wanting to break anything. It was like hugging a bird with its hollow bird bones, and Harper imagined she could feel her grandmother's bird heart beating inside her chest.

"How are you feeling?"

"Lazy," her grandmother replied. "Lazy and bored."

"Have you eaten breakfast?"

"Now you sound like the nurses. Who cares if I've had breakfast? When I'm hungry, I'll eat. It's not like the kitchen is going anywhere."

"You need to eat to help balance your medications."

Her grandmother tsked and waved a fluttering hand at her. Harper pulled the blanket over Grandma Spurling's feet and tucked it beneath her heels. Harper knew she didn't feel the cold much anymore but didn't like seeing her feet so exposed. If The Mom had been here, she'd have done the same exact thing. The Mom hated it when things were untucked.

"You have school today, don't you?"

"Yep."

"How are your classes going?"

"Good. Lots of homework, like always."

"How's the paper? Any hot stories?"

"I interviewed our groundskeeper, Mr. Cho. He's from Vietnam. He helped the United States during the war and had to move here after we lost. He says he misses his homeland. Sometimes he feels like he's in purgatory."

Harper looked out the window. Her grandmother had an east-facing view of the creepy pine forest that curled around most of Hawthorn.

"You want purgatory, try spending every day in this place," Grandma Spurling said. "The highlight of the day is bingo in the sunroom, and half the players fall asleep by their second card. I'm thinking about buying one of those air horns and letting rip."

Harper smiled.

"Heck. I'd come to bingo to see that."

"Don't think I won't do it."

Her grandmother raised her bed with the remote so she was sitting up straighter.

"You have a boyfriend yet?"

"Grandma."

"What? A pretty girl like you, the boys must be hounding you day and night."

"The boys in my school only care about football, hunting, and their stupid trucks."

"And pretty girls like you, I bet. You just wait. One of them might turn into a prince one of these days. Watch out for the ones who seem a little different. They turn out to be the interesting boys."

"All right, Grandma. I'll keep an eye out."

"Good."

Harper sat down in the recliner beside her grandmother's bed and tipped her head back. She felt like taking a nap. She could fall asleep right here and wake up for lunchtime in the cafeteria. She didn't mind bland food or drooling table companions. It couldn't be any worse than high school.

"I was just watching the news," Grandma Spurling said. "They've found another body on the riverbank."

"They did?"

"It was a woman this time. She was young."

"God," Harper said, pinching the bridge of her nose. "What is that? The third river body in the past six months?"

"Fourth. They're not sure if this one was a murder or suicide. She'd been in the water for days, they said. The fish had been at her."

Harper opened her eyes and stared at her grandmother. Maybe this was why she'd woken up so early. Maybe Harper had sensed the discovery of a new river body all the way from across town and it had set off her mystical reporter senses.

"What's wrong with this town, Grandma?"

Harper's grandmother laced her hands together and set them on her stomach. "Well," she said, "Hawthorn has always been troubled."

The Wolves
(1857)

Sofie Helle lay awake in the back of her family's wagon, listening to the piping crickets and the wind rustling the high prairie grass. Cozied up in quilts on the wagon's wood plank floor, Sofie's mother slept on one side of her and her older sister, Gerta, slept on the other. It was a soft summer night, as deep as any, but Sofie had a restless feeling in her heart. She always felt restless. At seven years old and the youngest in the Helle family, she could not remember her birth country of Norway. For as long as she could recall, she had been traveling—first across a dark and vast ocean, then by train, and then finally by wagon, which was drawn by four strong oxen that smelled like dung.

Sofie's family had departed the city of St. Louis the previous May, one wagon among a small train of five. It had been a peaceful journey across the open plains, but lately, as a line of mountains appeared to the south, wolves had appeared to harry the wagon train. They'd appeared two weeks previously as a cluster of gray, trotting shapes set against the heat-blighted landscape, hovering beyond rifle range during the day and howling en masse during the long prairie nights. Sofie was thinking about the wolves—how hungry they must be, how their rough fur would feel to the touch—when a woman's scream pierced the night and caused Sofie to bolt upright, her heart thumping. She knew what the scream meant.

"Wolf, Mama! Wolf!"

Sofie's mother and sister scrambled to wakefulness inside the darkened wagon. Rifle shots cracked loudly, and a man shouted something in an angry voice. By the time the Helle women emerged from the wagon, a single wolf was already loping back into the night with something dangling from its jaws. Sofie's father, Torvald Helle, was running after the wolf with his rifle raised. He fired two more times and pulled up at the edge of the firelight, his body stiffening. To Sofie's left, Mrs. Hawthorn was being restrained by her husband as she writhed and screamed and fought to run off. She was calling for William, the Hawthorn's eight-month-old baby boy.

Sofie's mother wrapped one arm around Sofie and another around her sister and pulled them both against her waist.

"My Lord," she said. "It took William."

Sofie's father turned and looked back toward the camp, his head slumping as if he'd been struck with a club.

He'd been the lone man on watch.

———

Daylight found the settlers' wagons loaded and on the move, with a few men on horseback gone ahead to scout while the oxen pulled their heavy loads. The children were unusually sedate as the morning went along, either sleeping in the back of the trundling wagons or talking quietly among themselves, trading the colorful stones and flint arrowheads they'd picked up along the trail. Mrs. Hawthorn had passed out from exhaustion, and two of the other wives sat with her in the Hawthorns' wagon, the long needles in their hands clicking faintly as they knitted.

Sofie Helle sat in the rear of her own wagon, swaddled in a blanket but wide awake, watching the wolves in the distance with wide eyes. Unlike everyone else, she'd enjoyed their hovering presence. She'd howled back softly to them when they'd howled, as if they were having a secret conversation, and she felt betrayed by the baby snatching in a new and sad way she couldn't fully understand.

The wagon train halted at midday. The mountain line to the south they'd been following for the past two weeks appeared more defined, with a shadowy line beneath it that looked like woodland. The scouts on horseback returned to eat lunch with wide smiles. They'd found a clear river and a dense outcropping of trees the train could make by nightfall. It would be a fine place to make camp, a fortified location where they could stay all winter.

The other settlers took this news with grave impassivity, slowly absorbing the idea that their arduous journey could be so nearly ended. Sofie walked to the back of the wagon train and looked to the north. The wolves were lying out in the grass, ten or twelve gray shapes cooling their bellies and patiently watching like army spies. One of the wolves shifted, tossing some flailing, meaty thing into the air and snatching it up again in its jaws, as if toying with it. Sofie felt a spell of warm dizziness pass over her. Only a rabbit, she told herself, or some other unlucky furred creature of the prairie.

————

The settlers reached the forest with an hour of daylight left. After the vast seas of prairie grass and open blue skies, the dense woods appeared to promise an abundance of interesting things, like mule deer and elk and berries and cool dark spots for hiding. Sofie whistled to the birds flitting about the canopies, and the birds whistled back. Branches rustled. A doe appeared between two juniper shrubs, looked out at the group, and ran off again before anyone could think of lifting a rifle.

Sofie squinted at the thick woods. The many lush shades of green, now darkening as the sun went down, appeared to blend in an uncanny way. The wagon train curled around the edge of the forest and headed east. To the south, mountains now dominated the horizon, while more flat prairie opened to the west.

Sofie heard the river before she saw it. Running fast and deep at the bottom of a steep grassy bank, the river tumbled out of the forest like a surprise and wound south across an open plain for several miles before disappearing into more woods. On the other side of the river was a mile or so of tall grass that abutted the eastern tree line. The settlers parked the wagons along the riverbank, and everyone disembarked except Mrs. Hawthorn, who was still asleep in the rear of the Hawthorn wagon. A gentle slope was found along the bank, and everyone filed down to the river, the children skipping ahead and dipping their toes into the current. The adults knelt along the shore as if in prayer and scooped water over their heads, washing away the day's heat and the night's terrors.

Sofie also knelt by the river and splashed the cold water on her face, careful to mind her balance and not fall in.

This was it, she realized.

This place would be their haven.

2

HARPER LEFT BURBLING Brook after she got Grandma Spurling to promise she'd get out of bed and do something with her day. Harper was worried her grandmother was getting depressed, and she wished her grandfather was still alive. Grandpa Spurling had been a funny, sweet guy, kind of like a happy elf with twinkling blue eyes, and he could cheer anyone up. He'd died of a stroke three years earlier while he was taking a shower. He'd been singing show tunes, like he always did in the shower, and Grandma Spurling said he'd stopped right in the middle of "Oh What a Beautiful Morning" and she heard a hard THUNK as he fell in the tub, already dead.

Though she was as stunned and heartbroken as anybody, Harper had helped her mother write her grandfather's obituary and even the speech The Mom gave at his funeral. Writing about Grandpa Spurling had made Harper feel sad, but kind of good, too, like she'd done something meaningful. She realized that if you didn't write things down, if you didn't document what was going on in the world, the important stuff could easily be lost and forgotten. She started reading news websites. She joined the school paper and started writing about current events, big and small. She began paying closer attention to everything that went on around her, looking for a fresh angle, a story nobody else was talking about.

The world had layers, she'd discovered.

A lot of layers.

Harper drove past Hawthorn High and turned into the big gravel parking lot behind it. Cars and trucks were still pulling in, thumping music and throwing up clouds of gravel dust, and Harper almost got hit by an asshole in a green jeep who zoomed right past her car as if it was invisible.

The asshole was her best friend, Eva Alvarez.

"Mother fuck."

Harper turned the wheel hard and followed Eva's jeep across the parking lot. Eva pulled into a spot at the back of the lot, where she always liked to park, and Harper parked her car right beside her. She grabbed her backpack, got out, and slammed her door, already throwing shade at her best friend, who grinned and waved at her from inside the jeep.

"You almost hit me!"

Eva made a derp face and laughed. She had a sucker in her mouth even though it was only eight in the morning. Harper sighed, opened the jeep's passenger door, and sat down with her backpack in her lap.

"What the hell, Eva? You almost smashed into my car."

Eva twirled the handle of her sucker, spinning it inside her mouth. "I don't know what you're talking about, Harp. I was driving like super normal."

"Yeah right. You're freaking crazy."

Eva rolled her eyes and popped the sucker out of

her mouth. She offered it to Harper and smiled, batting her long movie-star eyelashes.

"Here. Peace offering."

"Thanks, but hard pass on your nasty sucker. How can you eat that so early? Your mouth is going to taste funky all day."

"It's an edible."

"What?"

Eva ginned.

"You heard me, lady."

Harper took the sucker and sniffed it. It did smell a little strange.

"This has pot in it?"

"My bro gave a couple to me for doing his laundry. He had a mountain of fucking laundry. Trust me, he got a good deal. His sheets were gross as shit."

Harper licked the sucker. It made her tongue tingle.

"Holy cow."

Eva nodded.

"Oh yeah."

Harper put the edible in her mouth and gave it a twirl. It tasted like cherry with a hint of beer. If Eva hadn't said anything, she wouldn't have known the difference.

"Edibles are really strong, aren't they?"

Eva looked in the rearview mirror, checking herself out. Half black and half Mexican, Eva had caramel-colored skin and big, brown eyes that made her look like a manga character. She had a short, pixie-style haircut and jet black hair. She was one of the most popular girls in school, but it somehow hadn't made her bitchy at all. In fact, Eva Alvarez was friendly to everybody and would happily dive right into any group and start chatting people up. Harper, on the other hand, preferred to hover on the edges of groups, agreeably nodding and asking only the occasional question—that way you could watch everybody and catch all the little details.

You couldn't listen when you were talking.

"Shit, I hope edibles are strong," Eva said. "I don't want to go through trig totally sober."

Harper took another lick and gave the sucker back to Eva. They left the jeep, crossing the parking lot and heading toward the school's rear doors. Eva kept stopping to say hi to people, and it took five minutes just to go fifty feet. By the time they actually got inside the school, Harper could feel the weed kicking in.

The school smelled like limes and coffee today.

Eva's hair was extra glossy.

She'd forgotten to ask Mr. Cho how much a school janitor made.

Had The Mom ever smoked pot? It was hard to imagine.

As they walked toward trigonometry, Eva leading the way like a friendly ambassador from Secret Stonerville, Harper noticed the way the hallway's florescent lights made everything glow and the bright purple and gold lockers really pop.

"Jesus, Harper," Eva said, smiling at her. "Wipe that goofy look off your face."

"What look?"

"Oh boy." Eva grabbed Harper's elbow and pulled her

into the bathroom, shoving Harper in front of a mirror. There she was, smiling at her own smiling reflection.

"See? You're totally obvious."

Harper made herself frown. She looked at her hair and twirled it around her finger. Eva was standing behind her.

"My grandma said I'm pretty," Harper said.

"You are pretty. I tell you that, like, every damn day."

"I know."

Harper sighed. Her little high was starting to fade already.

"You know what? Someday we'll both be old and gray and living in a nursing home like my grandma."

"Not me," Eva said. "I'm going out in a blaze of glory around thirty-five. I'm thinking a plane crash. You know, one of those private jets rich people have?"

Harper wrinkled her nose. She didn't want to think about Eva dying before she did. A good best friend waited for you to die first, so she could be there to cry and lament at your packed funeral.

"The bell's about to ring, Harp. You gonna be all right? I don't need you acting all cronked in front of Mr. Thiel and getting me in trouble."

Harper stared at her reflection. Was she all right? What did being all right even mean? Harper turned around and shifted the backpack on her shoulder.

"Did you hear about the woman?"

Eva raised an eyebrow, scanning her like The Mom usually did.

"What woman?"

"They found a dead woman this morning on the river-bank. They think she could be another victim."

Eva shivered. "Damn. The cops in this town need to get off their asses and catch this dude. I don't need to be stabbed before I go to college. I got plans."

"What do you think the Tender Heart Killer looks like?"

"Old and rape-y. Probably has one of those old-school porn mustaches."

"He can't be that old if he's killing people and dumping them in the river. He's killed men, too. You need to be strong to throw a grown man into the river." Harper crossed her arms. "You know, these murders are the only real story in this town."

"Sure, I guess," Eva said, glancing over her shoulder at the bathroom door. "But they're a little out of the *Hawthorn Squawker*'s league, aren't they?"

"Well—"

The bell rang and Harper jumped, even though she'd known the bell was coming. "Okay, lightweight," Eva said, pulling her by the hand. "Time for you to pretend like you're not stoned." They ran down the hall and entered Mr. Thiel's room. Everybody was still talking while Mr. Thiel wrote out formulas on the board, his back turned to the room. Harper sat at her desk and pulled her trig book and her binder out of her backpack. She fished around the bottom of her bag for a pen and a stick of gum. She decided chewing gum would help her concentrate better, but she couldn't find any. The boy who sat in front of her, a blond preppy dude named Kevin Osgaard, turned and said hi.

"Hi," Harper said, throwing it right back at him.

"You do the assignment?"

Harper thought about the question.

"Yes, Kevin. I did."

Kevin grinned like they were both in on a secret.

"Pretty easy, right?"

Kevin was always trying to talk to her. He was cute, in a boring TV weatherman kind of way, and really nice. For some reason, though, Harper could barely make herself be polite when they "chatted."

Maybe it was because his teeth were so white?

It could have been because his teeth were so white.

So.

Damn.

White.

"I'd say it was about the right amount between hard and easy," Harper said, scanning the rest of the room, hoping boring old Mr. Thiel would get started already. He was wearing the ugly brown tie again. That made three days in a row.

Well, at least he was reliable.

3

BY THIRD PERIOD, Harper had leveled out. She sat normally at her desk, feeling normal, during American History. The class's teacher, Mrs. Randolph, smiled at them from the front of the room as the bell rang, clasping her hands together like she was about to deliver a TED talk. She liked to torture you by always being perky and super friendly and making you not want to let her down by slacking off. Also, with her you knew whatever naughty thing you said or did would get reported back to The Mom, as if Mrs. Randolph was actually a reconnaissance drone who happened to look like a lady with poufy blond hair, good skin, and a big wide smile.

"Good afternoon, class," Mrs. Randolph said. "We'll start today by working on our diary entries." The class groaned, and everyone opened their notebooks. They'd been keeping diaries since the first week of spring semester. They'd read some famous diary entries like Anne Frank's and some other entries from a girl named Sofie Helle who'd lived in Hawthorn during the 1860s. Mrs. Randolph seemed to get a kick out of reading them aloud to the class.

"Dear Diary," Mrs. Randolph would begin. "Today was colder than yesterday. Snow came down in the morning but the sky cleared by midday. We saw a white rabbit hiding against the snow. The rabbit did not think we could see it.

When we told Papa about the rabbit at supper he said we should have shot it for stew but I do not think I would be able to kill a sweet rabbit like that. It had a little pink nose that twitched as if it could smell every scent on the wind."

Sofie didn't have a TV, a computer, or a cell phone. The poor girl sewed her fingers to the bone and had to listen to her mom read from the Bible like it was Netflix every night while her dad went off drinking across town.

Harper's own diary entries had taken a decidedly weird turn over the past few months.

February 4th,

So this is the first diary entry for class. To be honest, I've never kept a diary before. You'd think I would keep one, because I work at the school newspaper, but nothing in my own life ever feels as interesting as what's happening to other people. What really happens to me that's important enough to write down? History is the big events, isn't it? Nobody cares about the small events. The regular people.

So why should I write down what I had for lunch today? Or the fact that my little brother Sam still pees the bed even though he's seven now and that's getting kind of old for bed peeing? Will somebody be reading this diary in a hundred years like we're reading Sofie Helle's?

I kind of doubt it.

February 13th,

Today I went for a seven mile run and we had lasagna for dinner. Then during family movie night Sam and Cameron wrestled on the couch and Cameron fell off and bruised his elbow. The Mom made a big deal about it like always and The Dad got the ice pack from the freezer.

Also, I was thinking about Sofie Helle. Her diary isn't as dramatic as Anne Frank's or about an event as historically significant as the Holocaust. She was just a girl who lived in a frontier town. Does her diary matter more than mine because it was written so long ago and it's published in a book kids read in school? Because it's rare and makes good "source material"?

And if her diary does matter more than my diary, does that mean her life is more important?

March 10th,

Sometimes I think about old black-and-white photos from the olden days and how everyone in the picture is dead. Even the babies the parents are holding are probably dead, unless they're like a hundred and fifteen. Somebody is going to be looking at pictures of us some day and thinking the same thing. That girl's dead, that guy's dead, that baby's dead . . .

Eventually, pictures are all that's left of a person. It's all a matter of time and scale, right?

April 15th,

It's strange reading the diary of someone your own age. Like you might look up and suddenly see her standing across from you, mad that you're reading her personal private thoughts even though she's been dead for so long.

What would Sofie think if she knew her diary had been published and was being read by hundreds of students every year? Would she be embarrassed by having all her secrets revealed, or would she be happy to know she was still remembered? Do the dead even want to be remembered or would they prefer to be forgotten?

Maybe being remembered disturbs them, like somebody calling your name when you're deep asleep. When all you want is a couple of more hours.

May 1st,

Last night I dreamt it was 1860 and I was dressed in pioneer garb. I had on a blue cotton dress with white polka dots and a white drawstring apron. I even was wearing a bonnet!!! I could feel the bonnet's strings knotted under my chin, how they were scratchy and tight.

I was in a log cabin and I was churning butter. The fireplace had a crackling fire going in it and it was winter outside but it felt cozy and warm inside the cabin. A girl was sitting in a rocking chair near me while I churned the butter. It was Sofie Helle and she was knitting a sweater for my dad. She said she was going to give it to him for Father's Day. I could hear her knitting needles clicking as she worked.

Then I woke up.

Harper turned her notebook to a fresh page and tapped her pen on her desktop.

Mrs. Randolph was sitting at her desk at the front of the room and grading papers. She always wore nice cashmere sweaters, usually purple or pink, nothing too flashy. Today she was wearing dangling silver earrings that looked like curved moons. They reflected sunlight and sparkled when she turned her head. What was she going to think when she read Harper's diary at the end of the year? Would she tell The Mom, or would she keep the diary secret, like a professional psychologist had to?

Mrs. Randolph glanced up from her desk. Harper leaned forward and stared at her notebook. She smoothed the notebook's paper and felt its smooth paper-ness against her fingertips. She thought about Sofie Helle and imagined a winter day in the olden times. A whiteout blizzard. No school, no TV. Only her log cabin and the fire in the fireplace and her sewing in her lap and her family sitting all around her.

Harper bit her lower lip and started to write.

4

OLAV HELLE SAT in the back of his civics class and tried to pay attention. It was hard, mostly because his teacher, Mr. Harding, was so boring, but also because of the skull in his backpack. Olav could feel it resting at his feet, thinking its skull thoughts.

We could cull him from the earth.

Olav shifted in his seat.

Oh god. Not this again.

It would be easy. His arms look weak and his stomach is plump.

Up at the front of the room, Mr. Harding said something about the responsibilities of being a citizen in a democracy. How everyone had to play a part and how the whole was only as strong as its individual parts.

I doubt this plump man has even killed so much as a rabbit, yet he is allowed to teach you? He is allowed to teach all these young hunters?

Olav glanced down at his backpack. He was starting to regret bringing the skull to school. All it ever did was cause trouble. Ever since he'd dug it up the previous November, there'd been nothing but trouble, trouble, trouble.

No. I have made you strong.

Olav nudged his backpack with his foot. Mr. Harding started erasing the marker board, which he always did when class was almost over. Olav sat up in his chair and looked around the room. Norwegian on his father's side and Swedish on his mother's, Olav's white-blond hair was closely shorn and his eyes were a bright Crater Lake blue. He was thin with bony shoulders, but he could eat an entire tuna casserole by himself and still feel hungry an hour later.

"I'd like to address one final thing, if I may," Mr. Harding said, turning around from the board. He was short and always wore checkered shirts with suspenders holding up his slacks, like a teacher version of a lumberjack.

"I'm sure most of you have heard about the woman they found on the riverbank this morning, yes?"

Everybody nodded. The whole school had been talking about it all day.

"Well, I just hope you keep this latest tragedy in mind this weekend when you're out around town. Make sure you let your parents know where you are and try to go places with friends instead of alone. If you see anyone suspicious, take a picture of them with your phone in case they try any funny business. We talk a lot about civic duty in this class, right? Well, part of your responsibility as a citizen is to report, and hopefully deter, crime."

Olav raised his hand. "Mr. Harding, how do you know she was murdered? It could have been a suicide. Or just an accident."

Mr. Harding nodded.

"Good point, Olav. We don't know for certain if she was murdered yet. I'm just asking everyone to err on the side of safety, okay?"

The bell rang. Everyone started to get up, and Mr. Harding wished them a fun and safe weekend. Olav picked up his backpack off the floor and slung it over his shoulder. The skull moved inside the bag, slumping against Olav's back. Olav tucked his civics book and notebook under his arm, not wanting to risk putting them inside the backpack with everybody else around.

"Hey."

Harper Spurling had come up beside him. Olav couldn't remember speaking to her a single time in his entire life. She had dark shoulder-length hair and brown, serious eyes that seemed to watch everything closely, like a hawk gliding over a field. He knew she worked on the school paper—he saw her name attached to some of the better stories.

"Maybe you're onto something," Harper said, smirking. "Maybe Mr. Harding knows the lady was murdered because he did it himself."

Olav glanced sidelong at Harper, trying to tell if she was kidding or not. He had a difficult time telling when other people were joking, or sad, or whatever they were being. Harper nodded over her shoulder at Mr. Harding, who'd sat down at his desk and opened his laptop.

"Can't you see him dumping a body in the Tender Heart?"

"Maybe," Olav said, though the image was actually absurd. "He could be stronger than he looks, I guess."

Harper laughed and headed toward the door, tossing her hair over her shoulder as she glanced back at him. Thrown off by the exchange, Olav waited until she was out of sight before exiting the room. The hallway was the usual madhouse of students shouting and slamming lockers and horny couples kissing each other like they had to share the same oxygen or they'd die. Olav stopped and watched Tim Kildar and Kendra Lane making out, studying them like a scientist. He'd never kissed anybody before.

Your thoughts are growing clouded, my friend.

Olav adjusted the strap of his backpack and felt the skull's weight shift inside.

You must keep your mind clear.

Tim grabbed Kendra's ass and gave it a hard squeeze. Watching this, Olav felt as if he could actually feel her booty himself. He mentally urged Tim to squeeze it again.

Or, better yet, reach between her legs—

"Mr. Helle."

Olav flinched. Mr. Harding was standing behind him, frowning with his arms crossed.

"It's not polite to stare like that, even if they're pawing at each other like animals in public."

"Sorry."

Mr. Harding looked up and down the hallway. More locker doors slammed shut as time ticked down to the next period.

"I have lunch now," Olav said. "Don't worry."

"It's not your lunch I'm worried about," Mr. Harding said, still watching him. "It's that look in your eyes."

He sees, the skull said. *He sees your true nature.*

"Don't worry, son," Mr. Harding said. "There's no rush

to get involved in all of that. It'll happen when it happens. When you're ready for it."

Olav backed away from the teacher, his face growing flush. Tim and Kendra had stopped making out and were watching him.

If only he knew everything, the skull said. *This soft man would tremble before you.*

"Yeah, okay," Olav said, turning away and hustling down the hallway. He kept his eyes on the shiny linoleum floor, unwilling to risk further distraction. He merged with the flow of students headed to the lunchroom and grabbed one of the beige plastic lunch trays like everyone else and stood in line. He tapped his lunch tray against his leg as the line moved along. He wondered what it would be like to run through the entire school with a machete, or a machine gun. What the lunchroom would look like splattered with blood.

Yes.

Their lives are yours to dispose of as you see fit.

Olav smirked, but he didn't reply to the skull out loud. He didn't want anybody to think he was crazy.

The First Winter
(1857–1858)

The wolves skulked around the settler's camp into September, howling sporadically in the distance, but by the time the Harvest Moon appeared, the nights had gone silent except for the occasional lone coyote cry. Sofie Helle enjoyed the tranquil autumn nights and slept deeply, snuggled in the back of her family's wagon beneath a heavy blanket. She was glad they'd stopped traveling and could make a home now.

The men went to work in the forest, felling trees and dragging them back to camp with ropes and oxen, where the felled trees were either turned into firewood or trimmed into building logs according to their suitability. Every able body, including Sofie, worked from sunup to sundown. They could feel the autumn air growing colder each day, and they had all heard the stories of settlers starving during the long American winters, the tales of men slowly growing mad as they ate their horses, their friends, and their families.

In the evenings, Sofie sat with her father as he smoked his pipe. Together they watched the sun set in the west, turning the horizon pink, then blue, then a fine, deep purple. One evening, Sofie asked him why such a fine place for a camp was so empty.

"You'd think a thousand Indians would be living here, wouldn't you, Papa?"

"Yes. I have wondered about that myself."

"Perhaps they haven't noticed it," Sofie said.

"No," her father said, frowning as he watched the horizon. "The Indians notice everything."

Sofie's forehead crinkled. "Well, perhaps they've been here but they didn't like it."

"That could be, I suppose."

"Perhaps this campsite is haunted."

Sofie's father glanced at her and puffed on his pipe, sending a cloud of smoke that smelled like burnt cherries rising into the air. A flock of honking geese passed through the evening sky, headed south. "The only haunts are in our hearts, I reckon," Sofie's father said, knocking the bowl of his pipe against his leg. "But those are real enough."

The first log cabin was fit for habitation by the beginning of October. The cabin's interior was a single open room with three small windows that could be sealed from within by wooden shutters. The joints between the cabin's logs were chinked with mud and straw, and the roof was built with boards and nails the settlers had hauled from the East, knowing how precious such materials were in the wilderness. By way of amenities, the cabin had a sleeping loft and an iron woodstove. The camp's women and children piled into the finished cabin at night and lay shoulder to shoulder, sleeping soundly beneath a roof at last and waking only when Mrs. Hawthorn had her night terrors and woke screaming for Baby William. The camp's men slept in the wagons, so exhausted they didn't even snore.

The settlers laid out the foundations for four additional cabins and a barn large enough to hold the horses and oxen. The entire camp was set in a line along the east side of the river, putting the west at their doorstep and the forest at their back. Their luck held, and the other cabins were completed by the time the first snow fell. By Christmas, each of the five families had moved into one of the cabins, and the bachelors were snug in the barn's hayloft, where they had a woodstove of their own. Sofie slept with her sister in their cabin's sleeping loft, her blond head resting contentedly on a plump goose-down pillow. She'd plucked the feathers herself, from a goose her father had killed with his single-shot rifle.

———

In January the temperature plummeted, and a series of blizzards swept through camp, piling up snow until it was as high as a man's shoulders and topped with a hard crust of ice. Sofie and her family spent their days digging out their doorway and clearing snow from their roof, making certain their chimney remained clear. They had plenty of provisions on hand and firewood stacked up; each day was simply a matter of keeping warm and listening to the wind howl outside. Sofie and her sister huddled by the fire and carved funny wooden gnomes while their father read the Bible aloud and their mother knitted.

Sometimes, when they could no longer stand being cooped up, Sofie and Gerta would bundle up and visit their neighbors. Besides a few winter colds, the greatest trouble in camp was to be found in the Hawthorn home. Mrs. Hawthorn had still not healed from the snatching of her child, and she'd taken to asking everyone if they'd seen Baby William. "He's run off to be naughty," she would say, shaking her head. "When I find him I will give him stern words."

The further Mrs. Hawthorn drifted into delusion, the more frequently Sofie visited the Hawthorns' cabin. She was fascinated by the adult's form of make-believe, which was not so different from her own, and listened intently as Mrs. Hawthorn spoke for hours about Baby William and what she thought he was up to now. Baby William was visiting Chicago. Baby William had joined the circus and become an acrobat. Baby William had gotten a job as a train conductor.

In February the weather grew even colder. Everyone wore every stitch of clothing they owned, lumbering about like great fat mummies, and slept as close to the fire as possible. (Among the children, nearly every quarrel revolved around jostling for space.) Even Mrs. Hawthorn began to notice the cold. She decided Baby William had wandered out of their cabin and gone exploring in the woods. She claimed she could hear him crying on the wind, hungry and cold and wanting to come home. To keep Mrs. Hawthorn from wandering outside, Mr. Hawthorn restrained her with rope, tying her to a chair. William wanted to come home, Mrs. Hawthorn shouted over and over, weeping. She could feel his wanting on the wind, if only the forest would give him up.

One morning the Hawthorn family woke up to find that Mrs. Hawthorn had freed herself and left the cabin. After a brief search, Mr. Hawthorn found his wife on the edge of a wooded valley, kneeling with her arms wrapped around the trunk of a tree, her cheek pressed against its rough bark and a blissful smile on her face. Her eyes were closed, her body was stiff, and her skin was the light purple of lilac blossoms.

For the rest of that first winter, Sofie thought she heard the ghost of Mrs. Hawthorn calling on the wind, searching in vain for Baby William.

5

AFTER SCHOOL HARPER went to track practice. She ran sprints with her teammates until she felt like puking, the sharp spring wind buffeting her and making her eyes water. Harper had run track and cross-country since middle school, when she'd first hit puberty and felt like tackling everyone in sight. Running made her feel stronger, more in control of all the emotions that rattled around in her head. The more she ran, the better she slept at night and the clearer her thoughts became. If she skipped a day, just one day, she started getting snippy and irritated, and if she skipped two she just felt wrong, as if she wasn't herself anymore. She did okay at meets, usually placed in the top ten, but she wasn't as hard-core or as fast as the girls who usually won. She wasn't interested in running a marathon.

For her, running was more about the meditation factor. When Harper ran, she became a monk, peacefully alone on a mountaintop.

She became a sparrow on the wind.

Harper drove home after track practice and found her little brothers digging in the kitchen cupboards like a couple of overgrown raccoons. She stood outside the kitchen doorway and watched them paw open a bag of chips, a box of crackers, and two string cheeses apiece, feeling like a sociologist studying a previously undiscovered tribe of savages recently released into modern-day society for scientific purposes.

"What?" Cameron said. He bit the stick of string cheese in half in one bite, chewed it twice, and swallowed.

"Nothing. I'm just trying to figure out what I'm looking at."

Sam stuffed a handful of rice crackers into his mouth and chewed with a goofy smile on his face.

"Where's Mom?" Harper asked.

"Upstairs in her studio," Cameron said. "Working, like always."

The Mom was a landscape painter. She sold paintings through the three galleries downtown and also online. Tourists all loved her paintings of the Clawhooks, and they paid a surprising amount of money for them.

"Well, I'm going to take a shower and do my homework. You guys play video games and don't do anything dumb, okay? Mom needs to work."

"We aren't dumb," Sam said, opening his mouth as he chewed and showing off a gooey orange mass.

"I didn't say you were dumb. I said don't *do* anything dumb. And chew with your mouth closed."

Sam wrinkled his nose and opened his mouth wider. Of course he did. He spent too much time with Cameron, who thought loud farts were the funniest thing in the world.

"Nice, Sam," Harper said. "Real nice."

Harper left her brothers to their snack pillaging and took a shower in the first-floor bathroom. After the shower she went downstairs to her bedroom in the basement, her body wrapped in one towel and her hair in another. She picked her way through the mounds of laundry on her floor and dropped onto her bed with a loud sigh, nuzzling into her pillow. She felt something hard beneath the covers and pulled it out. It was Sofie Helle's diary. Harper rolled onto her back and opened the book to a random page.

> August 19th, 1862
> Dear Diary,
>
> Papa and Mr. Spurling have hired Everest Hahn to work with them in the forest. Papa is fond of saying Everest "could work the water out of a well" which is one of the funny things Papa likes to say. Everest is a quiet fellow and quite shy around girls. He likes to hunt all day in the woods.
> I wonder if Papa thinks Everest and I would make a fit match when we are grown.
>
> Yours,
> Sofie

Harper raised the book to her face and inhaled. The diary even smelled old, though this edition had only been printed in the 1990s. She wondered who Sofie ended up marrying. It didn't say in the diary, which ended abruptly when Sofie was only sixteen. Maybe Sofie waited another ten years before she found her one true love . . .

A buzzing came from Harper's backpack, where she'd

left her phone. She reached over and dug it out. It was a text from Eva.

Let's go see the river tonight

?

Where they found the new dead lady. Let's go see the spot
   tonight

Seriously?

There's going to be a candlelight vigil and shit

Weird.

C'mon! You can report on it (:

Okay if The Mom lets me. I'll text you later

You better! No flaking

Harper set her phone on the floor beside her and tucked her feet beneath her. She'd never been to a candlelight vigil before. It would make an interesting story for the school paper, if anything.

She'd need to find some candles.

———————

Tonight dinner was chicken Kiev with brown rice and cheesy broccoli. It had the right amount of crunchy in the breaded chicken and the right amount of cheesy goo in the broccoli. "Nice job, Mom," Harper said, cutting off another slice of her chicken breast. "This is really good." The Mom took a sip of her wine (she always drank red wine with dinner, no matter what they were having) and studied Harper.

"You like it?"

"Yep. It's tasty."

"How very . . . unusual of you."

"What do you mean?"

The Mom glanced at The Dad.

"You normally hate my cooking."

"No I don't."

"Really? What about my meatloaf?"

"That's an outlier."

The Mom smirked and raised her right eyebrow.

"This chicken is crispy," Sam said. "What happened to it?"

"Things you don't even want to know about."

"Harper," The Mom said. "Please."

"We're glad you like the meal, Harper," The Dad said. "Your mother worked hard on it, as always."

"I like chickens," Cameron said. "They eat a lot of bugs. I wish we had a bunch of chickens in our yard."

Harper checked The Mom's glass from the corner of her eye, waiting for the level of wine to get a few inches lower while The Dad told a story about something that had happened to him at work. He was a hospital administrator, and when he told work stories he got all excited, gesturing with his hands and mimicking the people he worked with. He'd wanted to be a novelist back in college, where he met The Mom, and when he'd started working at the Hawthorn hospital he'd only been a part-time clerk who smoked a pack of cigarettes a day and wrote until three in the morning. The Dad didn't smoke or write anymore, but he still told a lot of stories.

The Dad finished talking, and Harper noticed The

Mom's wine glass was almost empty. It was time to swoop in.

"There's a remembrance vigil tonight for Jamie Stendhal," Harper said, looking at her mother. "Can I go to it, please?"

The Mom looked over and scanned Harper with her Momdar. Harper shoveled some cheesy broccoli into her mouth and chewed.

"Who's Jamie Stendhal?" Cameron asked.

"The woman they found today in the river," Harper said, swallowing. "The Tender Heart Killer murdered another person."

"They don't know that for a fact yet," The Dad said. "It's only speculation."

"Did you know Jamie?" The Mom asked. "She was in her twenties, wasn't she?"

"I didn't know her, but I feel really bad for her. No matter how she died. And I might write something about it for the *Squawker*."

"Who would you go with?"

"Eva. Probably some other friends, too. Everybody's going to be there. It's at eight o'clock. I'll be home by ten, I promise."

"How much homework do you have?"

"Not much. I can finish it before I go."

The Mom shared a look with The Dad. Cameron burped and Sam laughed, drumming on his plate with his fork and knife. Harper's brothers always got squirrely after about five minutes of sitting at the table, as if they each had a spaz clock ticking in the back of their minds.

"Okay," The Mom said. "Be home by ten."

Harper smiled.

"I will. I promise."

"Oh boy," Cameron said, looking around the table with bugged-out eyes and puffed cheeks. "Harper promised."

"Cameron," The Mom said. "Be nice."

6

WHEN HE GOT home from school, Olav Helle headed into the forest behind his house with the skull still in his backpack. He passed through the Clearing where the neighbor's cat was buried and kept going. The ground began to slant downward, and gaps appeared between the trees. Olav emerged from the tree line and stopped on the edge of a cliff that looked out onto a wide, bowl-shaped valley. The valley was filled with a bristling army of pine trees, all standing at attention, and a thinning mist sat along the tops of the trees. A large, predatory bird—a hawk, or maybe a peregrine falcon—soared in lazy arcs above the valley, looking for prey.

The Doorway is here somewhere. We will find it.

"You think so? We've been looking for half a year."

The stars will reveal its location eventually. Have patience.

Olav didn't know how the skull could see without eyes or hear without ears, but it could. It was magic. Probably black magic. Black magic was always the strongest, and the best way you could make contact with the dead. Olav had asked the skull about how it worked, but the skull claimed it didn't know. The skull said it had amnesia because it had been dead for thousands of years. It was ancient.

Death is a fog.

"Did you have fun at school today?" Olav asked, speak-

57

ing aloud now that they were alone with only the squirrels and the birds to think he was crazy. "I don't know why you even wanted to go, since you had to be in my backpack the whole time."

I do not mind the dark. Long have I dwelled in it.

Olav unshouldered his backpack and unzipped it. He took out the skull and pointed it toward the valley below.

"Which direction should we go today?"

The skull was silent for a moment.

North.

"All right." Olav shouldered his backpack and tucked the skull under his arm. He carefully started walking down the side of the valley, rocky scree crumbling at his heels.

———————

The skull had been murdered a long time ago, but its soul was still restless and could not find peace. It wasn't supposed to be buried in the Clearing—it belonged with its people in the forest valley, it had said, somewhere hidden that you could get to only through a single doorway. They'd been looking for the Doorway for six months, and sometimes Olav wondered if it existed at all, or if all their time hiking through the forest had been nothing but a big waste of time.

I sense nothing here.

Olav had been walking north through the forest for thirty minutes. He'd forgotten to grab a snack before the hike, and his stomach was starting to rumble.

"Should I turn around?"

This forest is a maze to me. I once knew it so well. I once could hunt inside it with my eyes closed and never touch a branch. The stars sang to me.

Olav adjusted the skull under his arm. He idly wondered what he would do if they ever found the Doorway and the skull was finally put to rest. What would he do with his free time? He could get a job. He could deliver pizzas.

Turn around.

"Are you sure?"

Yes. We've gone too far.

Olav turned around and headed south, using the western valley wall as his guide. He'd been messing around in the forested valley his entire life. If they ever found a hidden doorway, he was going to be as surprised as anybody.

———

By the time Olav got back to the house, he felt tired and annoyed by another useless search. When he saw his mom sitting on the living room couch and watching TV, he just kept on walking. Olav went into his bedroom, set the skull on the shelf in his closet, and collapsed onto his bed. He was getting one of the headaches he got when he didn't get enough sleep, which was most of the time, because he had bad insomnia that kept him up all night until it was daylight again and he could hear the dumbshit birds singing outside his bedroom window.

Olav put a pillow over his face. Sometimes total darkness helped. Sometimes pretending he was dead and sleeping forever helped.

He felt as if his brain was cracking into pieces.

Calm yourself.

"That's easy for you to say. You're dead."

Olav rolled off his bed and went to his closet. He reached into the back of the closet, beyond his pile of dirty laundry, way against the back wall. He pulled out a wooden cigar box and sat down on the floor with it. He examined the box from every angle, checking for signs of tampering. He'd found it at a garage sale for two dollars. The lid had a buffalo on it, fake-burned into the wood. At the time, Olav hadn't known what he was going to use the box for, exactly, but he knew it would hold special things. It looked like that kind of box.

Olav flipped open the box's lid and leaned forward as he examined its contents. A gold necklace with a small cross on it, the clasp broken. A man's watch, gunmetal gray. A woman's diamond wedding ring. A gold money clip still holding a tight wad of cash.

Your takings are fine. You have become a fierce warrior.

Olav removed the gold necklace from the box and examined it more closely. It had come from a woman he'd killed near downtown the previous Thanksgiving. The old woman.

Your first kill.

Olav had been out walking alone around eight o'clock at night. He'd dug up the skull two weeks earlier, but it still hadn't spoken to him yet. He'd been cooped up all day with his family, eating Thanksgiving food and watching Thanksgiving football he didn't give a shit about. He'd gone into his bedroom, looked around, and noticed for the first time with total clarity how shitty his bedroom was, how small and stifling his entire house was. All he had was a bed, a scratched-up dresser, and a ratty armchair he sat and smoked cigarettes in. The skull was now the coolest thing he owned by far—somebody could have thrown everything else he owned in a dumpster and he wouldn't have cared much. How had he lived like this his entire life? How had he endured all the shittyness?

His head splitting with a sudden sense of angry claustrophobia, Olav had left his house without speaking to his parents and stepped out into the night. He started walking, first past his block and then through his entire neighborhood. Instead of cooling off, Olav felt his rage building the farther he traveled through Hawthorn. He walked all the way downtown to the river boardwalk. The walk, normally busy with shoppers and strolling couples, was deserted except for one older woman sitting on a bench. She was crying, for some reason, and as Olav walked past she gave this pathetic sniffle that made his teeth grind. He kept walking, found a heavy rock on the riverbank, and circled back down the boardwalk, his thoughts growing hotter and hotter.

The woman didn't see him as he came up behind her, raising the rock high above her sniffling head. He decided she was about his grandmother's age. Boring and old. Another shitty person living in this shitty little town.

Yes.

You were a ghost out of the darkness.

He'd paused, waiting for a final sign, and when the lady pulled a tissue out of her purse and made a honking noise, Olav brought the rock down as hard as he could, cracking her right on the crown. She gave a little gasp and slumped forward, falling off the bench and rolling tits-up onto the boardwalk.

A vengeful ghost.

Olav went and stood over her, looking down. She was still breathing. She was wearing a puffy down coat and a gold necklace with a cross on it. Olav yanked the necklace off, and when he stuffed it into his pocket he felt his dick shift against his leg. He looked around, saw nobody anywhere, and unzipped his pants, whipping his dick out and pissing all over the woman's face.

She still didn't wake up, even when the piss went up her nose and collected in puddles in her eye sockets.

You had claimed her for death.

He zipped back up again, grabbed the woman by both hands, and dragged her toward the river. She wasn't too heavy. She didn't moan, and her eyelids didn't flutter. A drop of blood leaked from the corner of her mouth, and a lot more was running down her forehead, mixing with the piss. The river was about three feet lower than the boardwalk and still not completely frozen yet, though ice had formed along its edges. Olav slid his hands beneath the woman and rolled her off the boardwalk's edge. She landed on the weak ice, plunged right through it, and bobbed back up only once before sinking out of sight altogether.

And that was it.

Without thinking about it too much, or feeling too guilty, Olav had killed somebody.

And he'd liked it.

You have been called for great things, the skull said. *It was no accident you dug me up. The stars sought you out as a vessel for their will.*

The skull had spoken for the first time after he'd returned home from dumping the old woman in the river. In a whispery voice that sounded like dirt and dead leaves, its first hungry words were:

The Doorway.

We must find the Doorway.

Olav closed the cigar box and ran his fingers across the buffalo indentation. He could almost smell the buffalo in the room with him, feel its warm breath on his neck. How would it feel to kill something so strong? And, more important, how long could Olav wait until he killed again?

You must continue the killings, the skull said, staring down at him from its shelf. *Each one honors the stars and feeds their bloodlust. Each killing brings us closer to pleasing their celestial temperament.*

Olav stood up and set the cigar box on the shelf beside the skull. Like a lot of crazy shit the skull said, he didn't know what to say to that. Sometimes it was just best to pretend the skull hadn't said anything at all.

The Blue Death
(1860)

Sofie Helle began keeping a diary when she was ten years old and her mother gave her a thick, leather-bound volume of lined paper. "You are always chattering so much," her mother said, smiling mischievously as she handed Sofie a pencil. "I thought you could sometimes write your thoughts down and give our ears a rest."

Sofie wrote in her diary every day, usually in the evenings before the fire. She wrote about the woods and the camp and whatever interesting events occurred. It felt reassuring to her to put down the events of a day on paper where they could stay as fixed as the Clawhook Mountains. Sofie liked being able to flip through the diary's pages and recall something somebody had said or done weeks or months before, recorded for all time, undeniable and clear. If her earliest memories all revolved around travel— their ship crossing the ocean, their train roaring toward St. Louis—her diary provided evidence that her family had put down roots and would not be floating off anytime soon.

The population in camp grew swiftly as more settlers arrived from the East. Sofie's family now had many friends and neighbors. They went to church each Sunday. They kept their cabin clean and tended a large garden in their backyard. Sofie's father worked a patch of the large forest with his friend Daniel Spurling, hauling raw timber back to town and selling it to the waves of settlers that arrived daily—one day soon they planned to open a lumber mill right along the river.

The camp even had a name now: Hawthorn, in memory of Mrs. Hawthorn and the wolf-snatched Baby William.

The camp was becoming a town.

———————

A few months after Sofie started keeping her diary, cholera swept through Hawthorn. It struck the Helle family along with everyone else, laying both Sofie's mother and sister low while Sofie and her father changed their chamber pots and fetched them water. On the third day of the outbreak, Sofie was sent by her father to buy whiskey. Her own stomach had grown queasy, but she could not decide if that was from the sickness itself or the rank fishy smell that now pervaded the entire town. Sofie bought two bottles of whiskey at the general store and headed straight home, uncorking one of the whiskey bottles as she walked and taking three deep pulls that scorched her throat and stomach.

Back at the cabin, she found her father vomiting outside their front door. When he'd finished, she handed him the open bottle of whiskey. He took a small drink from the bottle and immediately vomited again. Sofie went inside the cabin and uncorked the second bottle. Her mother and sister were lying on their bedding by the cabin's stove, bathed in sweat as they stared at the ceiling with dull eyes. Sofie made them sit up and hold their sick buckets between their legs. Their eyes remained dull and could not properly focus on her. She poured the whiskey into a tin cup and bade them drink, one after the other. They coughed and heaved and vomited into their sick buckets, their eyes watering with tears.

"Is this poison, Sofie?" Gerta asked. "Are we to die?"

"No, it's spirits," Sofie said, refilling the cup. "Drink again."

Her mother and sister drank and sputtered, their faces puckering, but this time they both kept the whiskey down.

"The whiskey will burn off the sickness."

Sofie refilled the tin cup and corked the bottle. Her father came into the cabin, sat down beside the sick women, and began wiping their foreheads with a towel. Gerta belched and set aside her sick bucket.

"I feel sleepy."

"That's fine, that's fine. Rest now. I will fetch water from the river."

Gerta lay back down and giggled.

"The cabin is spinning, Papa."

"I don't doubt it."

Sofie's mother shook her head and lay down as well. "A drunk child. We can only be glad your mother is not here to see this."

Sofie's father leaned down and kissed her mother's forehead.

"Do you know what they call cholera, Papa?" Sofie asked. "The Blue Death."

"Is that so?"

"They say you turn so pale your skin turns blue."

Her father picked up the well bucket and peered at the scrim of water at its bottom.

"Is my skin blue yet, Papa?"

Her father looked at Sofie.

"No, my lamb. It is not."

"Good. I am not done writing my diary yet."

Her father smiled, and Sofie could see how weak he was growing. She handed him the tin cup of whiskey and took the bucket.

"You lie down, Papa. I'll fetch water from the river."

"Sofie . . ."

"Go ahead. I'm still fit."

Sofie's father sighed and lay down beside her mother. Everyone was sick now except her; she would play nurse. Sofie left the cabin and walked swiftly down to the river. She found many of her neighbors on the riverbank, scooping up water and in many cases drinking from the river directly, lying on their stomachs and submerging their heads. Men, women, and children all, some of them defecating as they drank with their pants pulled down to their ankles or their dresses hiked up above their waists. The air swarmed with river gnats and horseflies, and the smell . . . it was a scene to behold, that was for certain.

Sofie walked north along the river, wanting to get as far upstream as possible, and found her own legs growing weak beneath her. She passed the last few cabins and came to the forest's edge, where she scooped a bucketful of water at the exact spot where the river emerged from the forest, as pure as it got. She turned back to town with her water-heavy bucket, no longer following the river but weaving through the streets, which were quiet and empty except for the occasional figure carrying a bucket much like her own. She found her family all asleep on the floor, and she set the bucket down at their feet. The weakness that had been nipping at her heels finally caught up to her. Her legs buckled, and she dropped to the floor, passing out after briefly noting the cabin floor's coolness against her cheek.

———————

Sofie woke to clarity three days later, lying in her parents' bed and as weak as a newborn. Her father was holding a cup to her face, forcing her to drink water. She sputtered and choked the water down, unable to so much as lift herself into a sitting position, and her father smiled to see the recognition in her eyes.

"Finally you're awake. Good."

The water trickled through her. Her throat felt swollen, and her entire body ached as if she'd been beaten with a club.

"Mama and Gerta?"

"They're getting more water from the river."

Sofie licked her chapped lips, allowing the words to reassemble in her mind until they made sense.

"Twelve people have died," her father said. "Little Penny Spurling passed on the first night."

Sofie swallowed.

Oh, no. Loud Penny was dead.

"You'll be fine, sweetheart," Papa said, patting her forehead with a damp cloth. "Mama says the fever broke and you won't be turning blue."

Sofie stared at her father for a long while. She noted the birds whistling outside, their song like a musical allowance to return among the living.

"Can I have my diary, Papa? I need to catch up."

Her father smiled and patted her hand.

"Yes, daughter," he said. "I will fetch it."

7

HARPER DID HER homework for an hour before she started to get ready to go out. It would be cold by the river, especially at night, so she put on a sweater, coat, and scarf. Even in the summertime, Hawthorn grew chilly at night—it had something to do with the Clawhook Mountains being so close and the town's high elevation. You always had to be thinking about the weather and how fast it could change. If you didn't wear layers, it usually came back to bite you on your freezing ass.

At 7:40, Harper got a text from Eva that said outside. She grabbed her trusty moleskin notebook and a pen and stuffed them into her shoulder bag. She left her bedroom and headed out through the front door. "I'm leaving," she shouted, slamming the door behind her before anybody could respond. Eva's jeep was parked along the curb in front of the house, its engine rumbling as it idled. Harper crossed the yard and let herself into the jeep's passenger side. She looked back at her house, which was brightly lit against the dark night.

"Hey, Harp. You ready to get your vigil on?"

Harper unzipped her coat a few inches.

"A reporter never stops reporting."

"You got that right," Eva said, putting the jeep in drive

and pulling away from the curb. "And you're the most reporter I know."

Harper looked out through her window, scanning the houses. The Tender Heart Killer could have been inside any one of them. Biding his time. Planning his next violent kill.

"Everybody's coming tonight," Eva said.

Harper looked at her friend.

"Everybody?"

"Pretty much our whole school. Everybody loves a good memorial."

Harper checked her purse. The Mom had given her three white dinner candles for the vigil and an Aim 'n Flame. The Mom didn't know Harper carried a lighter in her purse for cigarettes and joints, which she never bought herself but just bummed from Eva or whoever.

"They do?"

"Oh, yeah. Vigils can be pretty hot. All that death in the air, you know? It's sad, but if you weren't, like, best friends with the dead person, it can be a good kind of sad. Like you start thinking about dying yourself and how fast life goes by and you get horny thinking YOLO."

Harper snorted. Eva looked at her cell phone, which was always buzzing. Harper estimated her best friend spent about fifty percent of her waking life texting, whether she was driving or at the movies or at a party. She'd text with people who were standing right in front of her. She could thumb a text while she maintained eye contact with you, like her brain and fingers were melded to her phone.

"A vigil's way better than a funeral, too," Eva said, still

texting while she drove and chewed gum. "Only the coolest types of death get a vigil. Like teenagers or heroes or murderers who are getting executed. Nobody has a vigil for an old fart who fell in the shower. Unless it's the pope, I guess."

Harper took out her notepad, turned to a fresh page, and wrote:

Vigils can be emotionally charged; possibly sexual?

Vigils are usually for young people, heroes, or criminals facing execution.

Vigils remind us of our own deaths and their imminent possibility.

"Hey," Eva said, lowering her phone. "Check it out."

They were still several blocks from Tender Heart Park, but the streets were already congested with parked cars and people walking toward the river. Eva pulled up behind a truck and parked the jeep in the last empty space on the block. Harper slipped her notepad and pen back into her purse, and they joined the crowd walking toward the park. The night sky was cloudy. Nobody was talking much, and it was a little weird, walking quietly with so many people. Harper zipped her coat up to her chin, huddling against the cold spring wind. She could smell the river's mineral fishy odor and feel its presence flowing past them before she could see it. As they neared the park, the string of little restaurants and local shops that lined Hawthorn's center thinned out and finally ended altogether, replaced by trees and the occasional bench. A hundred pinpoints of mellow candlelight flickered in the distance. The vigil in Tender Heart Park had already begun.

"Shit," Eva said. "I forgot a candle."

"I brought extra." Harper opened her purse and took out the candles, handing one to Eva.

"Thanks, Harp."

"I knew you'd forget."

Eva laughed, a sharp sound in the quiet night. Some grownups looked at them and frowned, already getting their vigil-serious faces on. They reached the edge of the park, and two girls emerged from the crowd and walked toward them. It was Carrie Ballard and Staci Wand, two girls from their grade. They both carried lit candles, and the candle glow made them look like characters in an old painting.

"Hey," Carrie whispered.

"Hey," Harper whispered back. She wondered if she should go ahead and light her candle now or wait until they reached the main crowd.

"So it's started, right?" Eva asked in her regular loud voice.

"Yeah," Staci whispered. "Her whole family is here."

Harper decided to just go for it and light her candle right there. She lit Eva's, too, and now they all suddenly looked a lot younger, like kids huddled around a campfire telling spooky stories while animals rustled through the surrounding forest. They walked across the lawn and joined the other people holding candles (Vigil-ers? Vigilants?).

"There must be a hundred people here," Harper whispered.

"Definitely," Staci whispered, nodding. "Probably more than that."

"Nobody ever gets together in this town," Eva said. "I guess it takes an old-fashioned serial killer to get people to hang out these days."

Harper hung back as people in the crowd eyed Eva. Carrie Ballard hung back with her, looking sad and tired, as if she hadn't slept for a week. Carrie had red hair and freckles on her nose that stood out even in candlelight. She was always making bowls and mugs in the school's art room and giving them away. She wanted to open a pottery studio after she graduated.

They stopped in the middle of the crowd and looked around. Where did you stand in a vigil for the best view? Anywhere? All the flickering candles made Harper think about Italy and that open area where everyone gathered outside of St. Peter's Basilica in Vatican City. That was called a piazza, right?

"This is so sad," Carrie said. "Jamie was only twenty-four."

Harper did the math; the dead woman was only eight years older than she was. What would she do if she knew she had only eight years left to live? Eight years seemed like far into the future, past high school and college, but it would probably go really fast. The Mom was always saying how fast time went by as you got older and how every year sped up a little more than the one before it. "Just you wait," she always said. "One day you'll wake up and you'll be the uncool old person."

A wave of murmuring rippled through the crowd. On the side of the park facing the river a figure ascended a small podium Harper hadn't noticed in the dark. It was a man holding a candle of his own and a book. The podium had a small microphone, and the man tapped it as he leaned forward, revealing a priest's collar above his fleece jacket.

"It's Father Tanner," Eva said, looking back at Harper. "He's our priest."

The priest cleared his throat, and the crowd quieted. You could hear the Tender Heart River burbling in the distance behind him. The same river Jamie Stendhal's body had been floating in for several days.

"Hello, everyone," Father Tanner said. "The Stendhal family would like me to thank you all for coming out tonight. It means a great deal to them that you'd come down on a chilly spring evening to hold vigil with us."

Father Tanner cleared his throat again. It was hard to tell from so far away, but he looked as if he might be choking up a little.

"Jamie was a lovely young woman," he said. "In the youthful prime of her life, she'd just gotten her cosmetology degree a few months ago and was working at the Golden Locks beauty salon. She was a sister and a daughter and a good friend to many of you. She loved to ski. She loved to scrapbook and knit. She had a dog, Mylie, a little terrier that slept at the foot of her bed every night."

Father Tanner paused. The wind, which was blowing in from the west, picked up and caused all the candles to flicker and send shadows dancing around the crowd. Harper suddenly wished she was back home, burrowed beneath her blankets and all toasty, with her family thumping around upstairs.

"But Jamie has been taken from us," Father Tanner continued, "taken far too soon and far too young. Such was the Lord's will, which we may find inscrutable at times like this, if not downright infuriating. We live in a fallen world, given over to acts of wickedness. Given over to violence and murder and suffering."

The wind blew harder. Several of the candles were snuffed out.

"In the face of a trial such as this, we can only do our best to walk in the Way of the Light," Father Tanner said. "We can only support each other, support those who grieve the dead and pray for Jamie to find eternal peace. Pray for her soul to find its way to the Lord, who receives and gives succor to all those who have been taken too soon by the hand of violence. Please join me now in the Lord's Prayer."

Harper looked down at the burning candle in her hands and mumbled along as the crowd went through the entire "Our Father, who art in heaven . . ." spiel. Her family was Methodist, but Harper hadn't gone to church with them since she was thirteen. With all its crazy stories and prophesies, she thought the Bible was like a comic book for people who didn't have comic books yet (not to mention TV or the Internet). Also, if you combined all the wars and torture and general shaming organized religion had been involved in, Harper figured it would probably have been better if people skipped church altogether and just went for a good long run.

The short prayer ended, and Father Tanner thanked them all again for coming. He said the vigil would last twenty more minutes and everyone could feel free to share their remembrances of Jamie with each other or simply spend the time in reflection. Then the priest stepped down from the podium and they were all just standing around in the dark, shielding their candles from the nipping spring wind.

8

TWENTY MINUTES LATER, the vigil crowd began to break up and head home. Instead of heading back to the jeep, Harper and Eva walked farther south down the river with Staci, Carrie, and six or seven other sophomores, including a few boys. They walked on the river's wooden boardwalk, which went for two miles in each direction and was popular during the day with power walkers and parents jogging with strollers. Harper usually avoided the board-walk when she went running because it got so crowded, but tonight it was deserted.

"Well, that was a bummer," Eva said, lighting a joint. "Good speech by Father Tanner, though. Better than most Sundays."

Eva took a drag off the joint, held it a few seconds, and exhaled.

"You go to church?" Carrie said, fanning away the mari-juana smoke.

"Oh, yeah," Eva said. "My pops is hella Mexican Cath-olic. Makes us all go."

"We're Lutheran," Carrie said. "We only go twice a month, though. My mom says that's enough church for anybody."

"Shit, you all are going to hell," Eva said, laughing. "With my dad, if you miss one week you have to say, like, a thousand Hail Marys. Sometimes he wakes me up in the middle of the night just to check if I said my prayers."

"That's crazy," Harper said, accepting the joint as Eva passed it to her. "Your dad needs to settle down."

"Yeah. You're telling me."

Harper, Eva, and Carrie had fallen back from the rest of the group. Harper wasn't great at smoking and walking and talking all at the same time. She'd only started smoking the previous New Year's Eve, when she finally broke down and smoked clove cigarettes at a party at Eva's uncle's house. The Mom had bashed her over the head with the horrors of lung cancer ever since she was a little kid, and for a long time she'd thought just one puff would turn her lungs as black as tar. Harper hadn't really liked the taste of the clove cigarette, but she enjoyed lighting something on fire and watching a cloud of smoke rise above her head, as stupid and probably suicidal as smoking was.

The crowd ahead of them had stopped and were gathered at one spot along the riverbank. They'd walked about a half mile south of Tender Heart Park, and you could see a few dozen candles still burning in the park. Probably just Jamie's closest friends and family, huddled together and bawling their eyes out.

"God," Harper said. "This is all fucked up."

Carrie snorted, though Harper hadn't been joking. They joined the other sophomores by the river, and everyone looked down at the dark water. You could see a little curved wisp of sand covered by rocks and stranded deadwood running along the riverbank's curve.

"This is it," Staci Wand said, looking back at Harper. "This is where they found her body this morning."

"It's like you can almost see her," Harper said, "lying on that sandbar."

"I wonder if she was naked," Eva said. "Do you think the fish ate her clothes off?"

"Or the river current could have just pulled them off," Harper said. "That happens, right? Especially if she was underwater for a couple of days."

"God, you guys," Carrie said, shivering. "Morbid much?"

Harper took one more drag on the joint and handed it back to Eva. "People always say morbid like it's a bad thing to be." The other girls looked at her. Harper took a breath and felt the pot move through her bloodstream. "Morbid just means you're focused on death, right? Well, what if that just makes you appreciate being alive more? And, like, treat people better? Because you're thinking about how you won't live forever. I mean, we're all going down the river someday, if you think about it."

Eva smirked and Carrie hugged herself. "Maybe I don't want to think about it," Carrie said. "Thanks, though."

Two of the guys in their group started wrestling on the edge of the riverbed, trying to shove each other down the bank. It was another one of those spontaneous sophomore dude spaz moments that annoyed Harper so much. How could they have been at that somber vigil only ten minutes before and now act like this? It was like nothing ever really registered with them.

"I'm morbid sometimes," Eva said, kicking a rock down the riverbank. "Sometimes I lay in my bed and pretend I'm at my own funeral. I cross my hands over my chest and see how long I can hold my breath."

"I think that's meditating," Staci said. "That's like yoga."

Eva raised her chin, looking up from the river at the clouded night sky. "You should meet my Grandma Alvarez sometime. She's a straight-up sugar-skull-making *Día de los Muertos*-loving Mexican. She sees ghosts wherever she goes. She calls them her *amiguitos*."

"Amiguitos?" Carrie said.

"Her little friends."

One of the wrestling dudes lost his balance and slid backward down the bank. He landed in the pile of drift-wood, and you could hear a loud THUNK as the back of his skull struck wood.

"Devin?" the other wrestling dude said. "You cool, man?"

Devin sat up and rubbed the back of his head.

"You fucker, Matt!"

Harper sighed and shook her head.

"But by the grace of God."

The other girls looked at her. It was something The Mom always said.

"Know what the freakiest thing is?" Eva said, handing the joint to Carrie. "That killer dude is still out there. The cops don't even know what he looks like."

Devin got to his feet and scrambled back up the riverbank. He almost slid back down again, but Matt reached out at the last second and caught him by the arm, pulling him up and throwing him back onto the boardwalk.

"Why do you think the Tender Heart Killer is a guy?" Harper asked.

"You kidding?" Eva said, nodding toward Devin and Matt. "With freaky shit like this it's always a fucking dude."

Carrie giggled loudly, exhaling a white cloud of smoke. She always got giggly when she got high.

———

They sat on the riverbank for a while smoking and drinking vodka one of the boys had brought in a flask, and Harper lost track of time. By the time they'd walked back to Eva's jeep and she'd driven Harper home, it was already 10:52, almost an hour past when Harper had promised she'd be home. Harper patted her coat as she walked up her front walk, hoping to smack the pot smell out of it, and she chewed a piece of mint gum until her mouth felt normal-ish. She spit the gum back out before she went in the front door (gum chewing was a big-time giveaway, Eva said) and folded it inside its paper wrapper, dropping it back into her purse like a dirty secret.

She could sense The Mom waiting for her as soon as she got inside, of course. There was no sneaking in at the Spurlings'. The Mom stayed up as late as you did. The Mom worked at home, painting in her well-lit studio at the front of the house, on the second floor, with the view of the entire street laid out at her feet. She saw all and heard all. She could paint a mountain range and catch you sneaking out at the same time.

Harper got her possibly funky-smelling coat off and put away in the hall closet before The Mom reached the foot of the stairs, looming above her like a steely-eyed statue of justice. Harper could hear a World War II documentary blaring behind her in the living room, which meant The Dad was drinking beer and watching TV by himself. Sam and Cameron had been in bed since nine, though that didn't always mean they were asleep.

"Harper?"

"Hi, Mom."

"Do you know what time it is?"

"Evening time."

"It's eleven. You said you'd be home by ten."

"Oh. Sorry about that."

"Harper?"

"What?"

"Do we have to have this same old argument?"

Harper kicked off her shoes, sending them down the stairs in the general direction of her basement lair. She hated fights with The Mom. They were so boring and so annoying at the same time, like watching golf on TV while mosquitoes buzzed around you. Fights with The Mom gave Harper some serious eye-scratching feels.

"You could just be cool and let me be an hour late. I wasn't doing anything. We just lost track of time. And the vigil is going to make for a great story."

The Mom crossed her arms and gave her the Look.

"Here's your story. You're grounded for the weekend."

"Fine. I don't care."

"Great. You can help me clean out the garage."

Harper groaned and threw her head back. She hated the garage. It smelled like mildew and was sprinkled with mouse turds.

"How was the memorial service, anyway?"

Harper sighed and tucked a strand of loose hair behind her ear.

"Sad, cold, and windy. Lots of candles."

"That poor girl."

"Yeah. Father Tanner gave a good memorial speech."

The Mom stared down at her. Her eyes had gone soft, as they could sometimes without warning.

"Things like that are why I worry about you, Harper. The world is not always kind to young women."

"I know, Mom. I know."

They stared at each other another moment before Harper headed down the basement stairs, so exhausted she could probably sleep for a thousand years. She could feel her mother's gaze locked on her through the stairs and the walls, X-ray style, burning a hole into the back of her head. She wasn't called The Mom for nothing.

9

AN HOUR AFTER he returned from hiking in the valley, Olav heard his father's truck rumble into their driveway as he sat in his bedroom. His father, Anders Helle, worked as a roadkill removal specialist for the county. Every weekday he scraped the mangled carcasses of deer, fox, skunks, dogs, raccoons, cats, and other unlucky animals off the streets and highways around Hawthorn. He wore special coveralls, boots, gloves, and a mask when he was working; by the time he got home at night, he was worn out, sticky with blood, and smelling like spoiled meat.

The Helles' house had a windowed front porch where Olav's father stripped off his outer clothes when he came home from work, right down to his T-shirt and underwear. He threw his outer clothes directly into a washing machine that was used only for his work stuff and washed them with color guard bleach. He had three sets of work clothes, but they wore down fast and he was always complaining about buying new ones, which he had to pay for himself.

When Olav was younger and had nothing better to do, he had sometimes tagged along with his father while he worked. He'd enjoyed riding around in his father's county work truck, with its big diesel engine and flashing orange hazard lights, sitting up high in the truck's padded leather passenger seat. At first Olav had only sat and watched his father scrape up all the dead animals and blast the road with a water sprayer, reducing the deep red bloodstains they'd left behind to a light pink, but as he got older, Olav started scraping up the carcasses himself, wearing his own mask and gloves as they scoured the county's highways clean of bloody fur, maggoty guts, and severed deer legs. He enjoyed pitching in and working as a team with his father, and he wasn't bothered by the job's gruesome nature. He thought all the ways an animal's body could contort itself in road-side death were interesting, offering up an endless variety of gory, vivid arrangements, each one as unique as a snowflake.

For lunch on workdays, they'd drive onto a forest road or a patch of uncultivated government land and eat in the truck's cab, devouring ham sandwiches Olav's mother had made and drinking ice-cold soda from his father's cooler. They didn't listen to the radio (they both hated the radio, especially the commercials), but they'd roll down the truck's windows and listen to the birds singing, letting wind blow through the cab and chase away the worst of the rotting meat smell, which always made Olav's mouth taste like copper.

These occasional workdays with his father stopped when Olav was twelve and some gawking busybody complained about Olav to the county. Olav's father was reprimanded for having a minor with no training tagging along on dangerous highway work and told he couldn't bring Olav again. It was pure bullshit, his father said. Pure county bullshit.

By then, though, Olav was kind of glad to stop helping

his father. The other kids at school were starting to call him Roadkill Boy, which wasn't exactly helping his popularity.

"Olav," his mother called, knocking on Olav's bedroom door. "Supper's ready."

"Okay."

Olav closed the cigar box with his kill trophies in it and put the box back in his closet, setting it on a shelf beside the skull. He waited, curious to know if the skull had anything to say, but it was silent. It even *felt* silent, which happened sometimes, like even the ghost attached to it faded away for a while and went somewhere else. Olav shut the door to his closet and left his bedroom, walking down the hallway past the living room and turning left into the kitchen. His mother was standing at the stove, and his father was already sitting at the kitchen table in his mesh house shorts, drinking a beer and smoking a cigarette. His mother was smoking a cigarette, too, while she stirred whatever was in the pot on the stove.

"Hey," Olav said.

"Hey kiddo."

Olav went over to the stove and looked into the pot. They were having mac and cheese mixed with broccoli and chunks of hot dogs.

"Awesome."

His mother took a drag on her cigarette and winked at him.

"Anything for my boys."

Olav drew a glass of water from the sink and sat down

at the table. His father was paging through a hot rod magazine.

"How many deer today?"

"*Dos*," his father said, holding up two fingers. "One doe, one young buck. Buck hardly had a rack started yet."

"Prairie dogs?"

"Four. They're getting dumber than ever."

Olav's mother banged on the pot with a wooden spoon and took out three bowls from the cupboard. She spooned out the food, piling the mac and cheese high, and set the bowls on the table. She took one last drag on her cigarette and stubbed it out. Olav's father stubbed his cig out, too, and everyone dug into their food. Olav was a slow, methodical eater. He went for the chunks of hotdog first, picking them off one by one, before digging into the mac and cheese, using the pasta to cover up the healthy green taste of the broccoli.

"Nelly Goodwin died today," his mother said, setting down her fork. "She passed right when I was changing her bedpan. I didn't even know it at first."

Olav's mother worked at Burbling Brook, a fancy nursing home south of town. She always had stories about old folks dying or wandering around the halls or even having sex with each other and then not remembering it the next day. She said she got proposed to about once a week and that she'd gotten real good at swatting away all the horn-dogs who tried to grab her ass. She'd worked there for fifteen years.

"That's a shame," Olav's father said, sipping his beer. "Nelly was a good one."

They finished dinner, and Olav helped his mother load the dishwasher while his father went upstairs and took a shower-bath. He'd take a shower first, to get the day's grime off, and then run the tub and soak in it for about an hour, smoking cigarettes and reading Westerns. He took a shower-bath every night, whether he'd been scraping animals or not.

"How's school, hon?"

Olav glanced at his mother, who was scrubbing out a pot even though they were about to put it in the washer anyhow.

"All right."

"You learn anything exciting lately?"

"Not really."

"How about girls. You get fixed up with a little lady yet?"

"No, Mom. Cut it out."

"I'm just saying. Handsome young fella like yourself should be beating them off with a stick pretty soon."

Olav sighed and dropped some silverware into the washer's loading basket.

"Hey," his mother said, "did you hear they found another lady in the river?"

Olav nodded. He remembered driving along the highway at dusk three days earlier, seeing the woman jogging alone in the middle of nowhere. He hadn't been thinking about anything much, but suddenly his hands had taken over, guiding the steering wheel so that the car clipped the runner's hip and sent her flying. Suddenly he was standing over her, pouring sand into her mouth as she lay unconscious in the ditch. She'd flailed some at the end. She'd been young and pretty, with her brown hair tied back in a sporty ponytail. He'd thrown her into the trunk of his car and driven fifteen miles north of Hawthorn, circling around the forest so he could dump her at a higher point in the Tender Heart River.

"Yep. They were talking about it in school."

"Poor thing. Her family must be tore up over her."

"I guess." Olav dried off his hands on a dish towel.

"They're having a memorial vigil for her right now in Tender Heart Park."

"That's nice. I'm going for a walk."

His mother nodded and bit her lip, still thinking about the dead woman.

"All right, hon. Don't stay out too late."

"I won't."

Olav grabbed his gray hoodie and walked out of the house, passing through the front porch as the washing machine buzzed. He pulled on the hoodie as he went down their front steps and stepped outside. It was still light out, but the sky was turning a darker blue and the sun had dropped out of sight. Olav headed east, toward downtown and the river. He liked to go out for a long walk every night, even when it was really cold out. He liked seeing people walking their dogs and doing lawn work and hanging out in their living rooms, watching TV. People were always more interesting when they didn't know you were watching them.

The river was eight blocks from his house. Olav didn't know why he was drawn to the river or why he'd decided to throw every kill into it. He didn't know why he was killing at all, actually, or why so far he'd killed two women and two men. Or why he didn't feel bad about the killings. Why he felt as if he was simply scraping up more roadkill and tossing it into the back of the county truck and nothing more than that, even though they were human beings. He could blame the skull for encouraging him, but he'd killed the first victim before the skull had ever spoken to him. The skull was more like his cheerleader, his trusted adviser, his positive reinforcement.

His second kill had occurred the previous December, when Olav had been hiking around the forest. He'd accidently discovered a hunter lying on his stomach in a deer blind, facing away from Olav and totally oblivious as he sighted his rifle on a doe. The hunter was hunting out of season, wearing all camo and no bright orange. Instead of saying hello, or heading in the opposite direction and leaving the hunter alone, Olav had picked up a heavy branch, crept up behind him on the forest's soft pine-needle-covered floor, and smashed the branch down on the hunter's head.

Again.

And again.

And then there was the businessman, back in February. His third kill. He'd been out driving around after school and stopped at the railroad tracks on the northwest side of town to wait for the next train to go by. Olav liked watching the trains pass through—that first whistle, far in the distance, the rumbling noise as the train approached, making the ground tremble—and he would pull his car onto the gravel access road that ran parallel to the tracks and park there, smoking cigarettes with the windows rolled down.

A train of chemical tank cars rolled through, and Olav counted at least forty cars. When the last car finally went past, a short fat man in a business suit was standing on the other side of the tracks, on top of the elevated incline. The businessman was crying, his whole body shaking, and his hands were balled into fists. He cried for a long minute before he noticed Olav watching him. He crossed the tracks and started down the incline, headed directly for Olav's car on his stumpy legs. Olav smoked and waited as the businessman approached his window. The businessman had stopped crying, but his nose was dripping snot and his face was all puffed up. Really, he was pretty fucking disgusting. Olav looked away and studied his car's radio as if he was considering turning it on.

"Hey kid. You like trains?"

Olav turned reluctantly toward the businessman.

"Yeah."

"Me too." The businessman leaned forward and set his hands on the windowsill. "You want to make some money?"

Olav stared at the man and took a drag on his cigarette.

"What?"

"If you let me give you a blow job, I'll give you two hundred dollars. Cash."

Olav blew a cloud of cigarette smoke into the businessman's face.

"Fuck. You."

The businessman blinked at the smoke. He stared at
Olav for a moment, his lower lip trembling, before turning
away and heading back to the railroad tracks. He walked
with his head down, as if he'd been defeated, and then he
collapsed and lay face down on the ground. Olav stubbed
out his cigarette and got out of his car. The businessman
looked so stupid, lying on the ground in a nice suit. Why
was he even out here on the edge of town? Olav gave him
a hard kick in the gut. The businessman coughed and sputtered but made no move to get up. His crying snot was
mixing with the dirt and becoming a smear of mud. Olav
kicked the businessman again and felt the killing heat rise
inside him. Olav was wearing hiking boots with stiff rub-
ber toes. He kicked the man even harder the third time and
heard a rib crack. The businessman groaned and rolled onto
his back, his eyelids fluttering. "I just wanted to make you
happy," the businessman said. "I just wanted to make someone happy."

Olav realized the businessman was insane, which was
weird. You didn't expect people in nice fancy suits to be
insane. The businessman should have been wearing dirty
rags and covered in pigeon shit. He should have been holding a cardboard sign with crazy rants about illegal immi-
grants or space aliens written on it.

"Please," the businessman said. "Just let me touch it,
kid. You'll like it, I promise."

"You need to shut the hell up."

The businessman sniffled.

"Please—"

"I said shut up!"

Olav kicked the businessman as hard as he could, landing the kick directly on the man's right temple. Olav felt the kick resonate through his foot, his leg, and all the way into his hip socket. The businessman's eyelids fluttered and then stilled, still half open. He sighed once, deeply, and his chest went still. He was dead, and Olav was suddenly standing over his third kill, stunned by its ease and swiftness.

The hard part had been lifting the businessman into his trunk, driving him north of town, and dumping him into the river.

That had been a real bitch.

———

Olav stopped walking. Several hours had passed since he'd left his house, and it was getting late. He was not downtown or near the river at all. He was on a quiet residential street he recognized from years of riding the bus to school. This was Brodigan Street. He was standing outside of Harper Spurling's house.

The lights were all turned on inside the Spurlings' house, illuminating their front lawn. He could even see a sliver of light peeking out from the curtains that covered the sunken basement windows. That could be Harper's room, right down there. He'd liked it when she'd talked to him earlier that day, after class. He could tell she didn't care if people called him Roadkill Boy. As far as he could tell, she didn't really care what anybody thought about her at all. Harper just watched everybody else and took notes and kept her business to herself. She was kind of like him.

The front door to the Spurlings' house opened and a man appeared, carrying a full recycling bin. He didn't see Olav right away, so Olav stuck his hands into the front pouch of his hoodie, leaned forward, and started walking as if he was just passing by. The wind picked up, carrying the earthy smells of dirt and pine needles with it. It was chilly, but not too cold out. All around town, people were settling in and getting ready to go to bed.

It was a good night to be out wandering and thinking about a girl.

Part Two

10

A MONTH PASSED, and the Tender Heart Killer remained at large. No new bodies washed up on the riverbank, and no new clues were found. Hawthorn was lulled into a collective forgetfulness as school ended, summer began, and snow melted on the Clawhook Mountains.

It was only the middle of June, but Harper Spurling was already having a strange summer. She didn't know what her deal was, but she couldn't stop reading Sofie Helle's diary or playing *The Oregon Trail*, an old video game from the 1970s. In *The Oregon Trail* you led your family from Independence, Missouri, to Oregon in a covered wagon, just like the settlers in the olden days. It was 1848, and nobody had cars or highways yet, so travel was hard, and you had to be prepared. You could be a banker, a carpenter, or a farmer.

Harper always picked farmer. You started with the least amount of money but had the opportunity to finish with the most points. You bought your supplies at Matt's General Store at the beginning of the game, and later on you could buy more at different forts. Harper always bought bullets, four oxen, one wagon axel, one wagon tongue, one set of extra clothing, two wagon wheels, and a decent amount of food. You had five people in your wagon party, and Harper usually traveled with Eva, The Dad, Cameron, and Sam (no The Mom, thanks). On the Oregon Trail, your party was always eating a ton of food and getting hungry. You had to ration your food and not eat too much. You could hunt for game, buy food, or trade for food with Indians. Some days you found berries, which gave you a little bit of food. Every day was just one hit of the spacebar, so you passed through the days fast. You wanted to leave Independence, Missouri, early enough in the spring so you got to Oregon before winter came and killed all the grass your oxen needed to eat, but you didn't want to leave too early, either, because then the grass would still be dead and it'd be too cold out.

Today, while sitting on the couch in the living room, Harper set out in the month of April. She hit the spacebar five times, and five days went by. She'd picked moderate for her party's pace because she didn't want to stop every three seconds to hunt for deer and squirrel. She'd played the game over and over again, but somebody always died and they had to bury them along the trail. The Dad got dysentery, Sam got cholera, or stupid Cameron got bit by a snake. Eva got typhoid a lot. Or the measles. Sometimes two or three people died when they tried to float across a river and the wagon overturned.

And sometimes things went really bad and the screen read:

Everyone in your party has died.
Many wagons fail to make it all the way to Oregon.

The Mom came into the living room.

"You're not playing that old game again, are you?"

Harper picked up the pace, pushing her party faster along the trail. They passed Fort Hall and kept going. It was late August. It was hot and dry, and the grass was bad for the oxen. Everybody was still alive, but their health was poor.

The food she'd purchased was running low.

A thief stole two oxen during the night, so they couldn't go as fast.

They found berries.

They broke a wagon axel, but they had one spare left.

The Dad got the measles.

She rested her party for three days.

It turned into September.

They ran out of food.

Harper went hunting but only shot a squirrel for two fricking pounds of meat.

The Dad died.

"Shit," Harper said, leaning back against the couch. The Mom was standing at the living room windows, looking out.

"What?"

"Dad's dead. He done got the measles."

"Really? He looked so healthy going to work this morning. I guess you're the other family breadwinner now, Harper."

"Can't work. Too busy."

"Right. Busy being a couch potato."

"I'm learning history."

"I played that game when I was your age. I don't recall learning much history."

Harper hit the spacebar again and again. Their party continued on despite The Dad's tragic passing. "There's a lot of deep stuff on the Oregon Trail," Harper said, frowning as thieves stole a wagon wheel and forty bullets. "You just have to dig for it."

"Right."

The Mom left the room. Harper continued to play the game out to the bitter end, losing Cameron and Sam to a river crossing gone horribly wrong. When the game was over, she closed the laptop and set it on the coffee table. She picked up Sofie Helle's diary and opened it to a random page.

> July 28th, 1861
> Dear Diary,
>
> Last night Gerta and I collected fireflies with Mama's lidded jars. We filled up two jars and carried them with us around camp as if they were lanterns. We walked all the way down to the river. We dipped our toes in the river. It was cool and I felt a fish nibble on my toes but Gerta did not believe me.
> Maybe I fell asleep on the riverbank for a moment and dreamt it?
>
> Yours,
> Sofie

Harper sighed and closed the diary again. She'd read it cover to cover a dozen times now and practically had the whole thing memorized. Mrs. Randolph would be so proud of her. Maybe she should call Mrs. Randolph and ask for some retroactive extra credit, turn that B+ she'd gotten in history into a solid A–. Maybe Mrs. Randolph could explain why Harper liked reading about Sofie's life so much and even dreamed about meeting her. She'd started looking at prairie dresses on the Internet, even bonnets . . .

The Mom came back into the living room carrying a basket of clean laundry. Harper couldn't prove it, but she thought The Mom did laundry only when somebody was around to watch her fold it on the couch like it was the hugest chore in the whole world. When Harper told The Dad this theory, he said she needed to learn to be more generous with people or otherwise she'd die alone in an apartment with ten cats and the heat turned off.

The Mom plopped down beside her on the couch.

"So. What are your plans today, Harper?"

"I'm going to catch fireflies in a jar and look up at the stars."

"Really? That sounds nice."

"I'm looking forward to it."

"It's only 12:30, though. You've got some time to kill until dark. Why don't you go outside and play with your brothers? Or take a walk around the neighborhood?"

Harper closed the diary and set it on her laptop.

"I knew you were going to say that."

"And I knew you were going to say that."

Harper stood up and stretched. "Fine. I choose walking over The Brothers. They're probably having a worm-eating contest right now."

The Mom smiled and folded a shirt on her lap.

"Yes. They probably are."

Harper carried her stuff down to her bedroom and changed into shorts and a tank top. She slathered sunscreen on her face, arms, and legs, and the smell of coconut followed her as she left the house. The sun was high in the sky, and Harper could feel its rays pouring into her head before she'd even gone down the front steps. Cameron and Sam were shouting in the backyard, their voices so loud and shrill everyone in town could probably hear them. She wouldn't have been surprised if they were spraying each other point-blank in the nuts with the garden hose.

What would Sofie want to do right now, if she were alive?

Get ice cream.

Everybody loved ice cream.

Harper crossed the street. They lived only two miles from downtown, and she could walk that easy. She checked her cell phone but didn't have any messages. Eva, who'd just turned sixteen the week before, was working at the grocery store all day, and the rest of Harper's friends were at camps or on vacation with their families. Harper was the big loser in her group, with no job to even complain about, so she was going to have to rock this ice cream mission solo.

Six blocks from home, Harper, already sweating and thirsty, realized she should have brought a water bottle and probably a hat. She kept to the shadiest side of the street, but even the shady side let in a blip of sunlight every five feet or so. She walked through the last of the residential neighborhoods and crossed a busy two-lane highway. She could smell the river in the distance. A car came up beside her and rumbled, matching her pace. It was a rusty silver car she recognized from somewhere.

The car's passenger window rolled down, and Harper could feel cold air-conditioned air pouring out. The passenger seat was empty, and the driver leaned toward the open window. It was Olav Helle.

"Hey," he said. "You want a ride?"

11

OLAV HELLE'S CAR smelled like cigarettes and pizza. The air conditioning was cranked to the max, and when Harper turned the fan vents toward her face it was like being blasted by the Swiss Alps in winter. Unlike most of the spazzoid boys in their school, Olav drove at a normal, safe speed, and she was able to kick back and relax while they coasted along, her sweaty back drying out.

"I was going to get ice cream."

Olav glanced at her.

"You know, downtown? At Mister Cone's?"

"Yeah. I know that place."

Olav turned his attention back to the road. He pulled up to a stop sign, braked fully, and looked both ways before accelerating through the intersection. Harper had never examined him so closely before. He was pretty cute, actually. He had a strong jaw and zappy blue eyes. Very Scandinavian.

Harper kicked off her sandals and flexed her toes. She needed to paint her toenails, but the chipped fuchsia looked kind of badass.

"I like your car. It's comfy."

Olav glanced at her again. He had a good Roman nose, too.

"I drive a lot," Olav said. "Since summer started I've been delivering pizzas for Panda Pies."

"Oh yeah?"

"I get decent tips on the weekends."

"Ha. I bet you meet a lot of crazy drunk people."

Olav smirked. "Yeah. They tip the best."

Traffic slowed as they neared downtown and old folks and soccer moms started hunting for parking spaces. Harper noticed the radio was off, and the only sounds in the car were the rumbling engine and the air conditioning blowing through the vents. Huh. Olav Helle must have been the only boy in Hawthorn who didn't feel the need to blast music when he drove like it was his own personal soundtrack.

They turned onto Jameson Street, which ran parallel to the western side of the river. They drove past Mister Cone's, which looked busy, and went five more blocks until they found an open parking spot. Olav put the car in park but kept the engine running.

"Sorry I couldn't get closer."

"No, this is good." Harper adjusted the strap of her purse. "Do you, you know, want to get some ice cream with me?"

Olav blinked and looked at her. His eyes were *so* blue.

"Okay."

Harper laughed, feeling weirdly nervous, and Olav turned off the car's engine. They got out into the hot sunshine, and in about five seconds, Harper was sweating again (or *glistening*, as The Mom liked to say). The boardwalk was filled with little kids messing around and summer tourists checking out the shops on their way to the Clawhooks.

Harper and Olav walked slowly, each trying to match the other's walking pace, and Olav looked straight ahead, squinting in the bright sunlight.

"Don't you have sunglasses?" Harper asked.

"No."

"Like, none at all?"

"Nope."

They walked past a gift shop. Harper touched Olav's elbow, which made him flinch.

"Wait a second. I'll be right back."

Harper ducked into the shop and bought a pair of cheap plastic sunnies and a pack of wintermint gum. She bopped back out of the shop and handed the sunglasses to Olav, who was still standing there squinting.

"Here you go. Now you won't get glaucoma."

Olav put the sunglasses on. Yep. He looked like a guy who'd honestly never worn sunglasses in his entire life.

"Better?"

Olav shrugged, his face blank. They arrived at Mister Cone's. The line to place your order was long, and the place was filled with little screamers smearing ice cream over everything while their mothers talked on their phones, looking fried. The air conditioning was blasting, but it didn't seem to help cool the shop down much.

"I think I'll get chocolate fudge smash," Harper said, reading the board. "Or strawberry cherry berry."

Olav bobbed his head, either acknowledging her or lost in his own thoughts. He was still wearing the sunglasses even though they were inside.

"What about you?"

"Vanilla," Olav said. "Two scoops."

Harper snorted. This boy was kind of amusing in a quiet, dorky way.

"Really? Vanilla?"

"Yeah."

"That's a waste of a flavor! At least get, like, French vanilla."

"Nope. Regular vanilla's the best."

They moved up the line and ordered their ice cream. True to his word, Olav got vanilla and Harper settled on chocolate fudge smash. They each paid for their own cone and decided to keep walking on the boardwalk instead of staying inside with all the screaming kids. It felt exciting to be walking with a cute boy out in public.

They found a bench that looked out at the river and sat down, their hips not quite touching but close enough that Harper could feel the warmth of Olav's body bridging the tiny gap between them.

Hmmm.

What would it be like to kiss Olav Helle?

Harper had kissed only one boy in her whole life, way back at her thirteenth birthday party. The party had been in her own basement with about fifteen kids from school (although she wouldn't have called them all friends, exactly). They'd decked the basement's big room with streamers and helium balloons, which had actually looked pretty cool, and The Dad brought down speakers that could plug into her phone so they could have music. Somebody had snuck in a bottle of schnapps, and it got passed around the basement after Harper's family went back upstairs. Harper had taken a big birthday pull from the bottle, and three songs later she was kissing a boy named Tyler Branch during a slow song. It was fun kissing him, but near the end of the song her stomach started to hurt and she puked birthday cake all over the front of Tyler's shirt.

Harper shuddered and bit into her chocolate fudge smash.

"Arg," she said. "Brain freeze."

Olav looked at her. Harper tucked a loose strand of hair behind her ear and looked at the river. A fish jumped out of the water, flashed silver in the sunlight, and dropped back again with a splash.

"Hey," Harper said, "can I ask you something?"

"Sure," Olav said.

"You know that diary everybody had to read in history class last year? *The Diary of Sofie Helle*? Are you related to her?"

"Yeah," Olav said. "She was my great-great-great-great-great aunt or something."

"Cool," Harper said, nodding. "So your family was one of Hawthorn's founding families."

"I guess so."

"Ours was, too. Daniel Spurling. He was a lumberman."

"That's cool. I like the Old West."

"I know, right? I really like Sofie's diary. She notices things most people never notice. Like how the smoke curls out of a chimney, or the way sparrows peck for straw to put in their nests. She's good at describing stuff so you can see it in your mind. She takes her time to give you all the details. When she writes about her dad's sawmill, you can almost smell the sawdust and hear the men shouting as they work."

Harper nibbled on the rounded edge of her wafer cone. A pigeon landed on the promenade's railing and stared at them, hoping for a snack. Olav bit a chunk out of his own cone and chewed it slowly, thinking. "I would have been good on the frontier," he said. "It would have been cool to live in a time with no laws or rules. Nobody telling you what to do."

"No doctors or dentists, either."

"I think I could pull my own tooth out."

"That's insane. You'd faint."

Olav snorted.

"I don't faint."

"You ever try to pull your own tooth out before?"

"No—"

"You'd faint, trust me."

Olav stared at Harper in an intense way. She smiled. "You could try whiskey, I guess," she said, scratching her nose with the side of her cone hand. "You could drink a shitload of whiskey, tie your tooth to a horse, and fire your gun in the air. The horse would freak out and take off. That'd pull your tooth out, I bet."

"Or I could just carve it out," Olav said. "With my Bowie knife."

"Ha. Gross."

Harper's cell phone buzzed. She pulled it out of her pocket and read the message. An idea popped into her head.

"Do you know Kira Fredrickson?"

Olav popped the last bit of his cone into his mouth and chewed.

"Uh, I don't think so."

"She's a grade ahead of us. She's got long brown hair with highlights? A silver nose ring?"

Olav shrugged.

"Well, she's having a party later at her family's cabin. It's up in the mountains. Like, thirty minutes away."

The pigeon, who'd been watching them this whole time, hopped down from the railing and started pecking around their feet. Olav kicked his foot at the bird, but it just fluttered a couple feet away and started pecking again.

"She says anyone's invited."

"That's cool."

"There's going to be a keg."

Olav leaned back against the bench and stared at the sun.

"Hey." Harper scooted down the bench and bumped Olav with her hip. "You want to go with me? To the party?"

Olav turned to look at Harper.

"It doesn't have to be, like, a date. Just for fun."

Olav nodded.

"Okay. I can drive us."

Harper smiled and licked her ice cream cone. Suddenly, her boring summer day had just gotten a lot more interesting.

12

AFTER OLAV DROPPED Harper Spurling off at her house, he reached behind the passenger seat and grabbed his backpack off the floor. He set it beside him on the passenger seat and unzipped it. The skull peered out at him from inside the bag, its vacant eye sockets dark and unreadable.

It is time, Olav.

"Time for what?"

The stars sing for another sacrifice.

"You always say that."

They are still waiting to show us to the Doorway. They seek appeasement. They seek more blood. We must show them our worth.

Olav groaned and rubbed his eyes. He was getting tired of fucking around in the woods and looking for a door that probably didn't even exist. Also, he was worried that he'd mess up the next kill and get caught. He didn't want to get caught. He didn't want to go to jail, even if he was only sixteen and still a minor. They might try him as an adult. He'd read in the paper how they'd put up new cameras along the river and increased the police force patrols downtown, especially at night. People wrote angry letters to the newspaper every week, saying how the cops in Hawthorn were inept and the town was unsafe.

They are sheep, and you are the wolf.

Olav put the car in gear and pulled away from the curb. Harper's house, and then her entire neighborhood, fell away.

She does not fear you. She will be easy prey.

"No," Olav said, glancing at the skull. "Not her."

Now is not the time for weakness.

Olav clenched his jaw and didn't say anything. He watched the road. Blood roared in his ears and his cock was hard. Spending time with Harper had gotten him all jacked up. He felt like he needed to whack off and take a cold shower STAT.

No.

He needed to go swimming.

"We're doing what I want to do. Period."

The skull didn't say anything, but Olav could still feel its presence filling the car, trying to bend him to its will. He turned back to the road and gripped the steering wheel so hard his knuckles turned white.

It was time to go swimming, simple as that.

———

Olav drove beyond the town limits and took an old gravel road into the forest. The road curled around the entire valley to the east—the same valley he and the skull had been searching since the previous November—and ran into the dense woods on the valley's opposite side. The gravel road had long been abandoned and was pocketed with holes. Olav drove slowly and did his best to keep his car from bottoming out. The half-mile drive took an intense fifteen minutes of cautious driving, but the challenge kept Olav from thinking about the upcoming evening or the skull with its psychic, pain-giving powers.

Eventually an old iron bridge appeared ahead, spanning the Tender Heart River. Olav parked his car in the middle of the road and turned off the engine. Nobody was out here. Nobody ever came this deep into the forest.

Are you certain of that?

Olav frowned and peered through the windshield. He noticed a four-wheeler near the base of the bridge, parked just off the road. He opened his door and got out of the car. He walked toward the bridge, stepping through alternating patches of shadow and bright sunlight. He made out the profile of a boy on the opposite end of the bridge. The boy, who looked about eleven years old, was holding a fishing pole and staring down at the water rushing beneath the bridge, lost in thought.

Olav stepped onto the bridge and headed toward the boy. He'd never seen anybody on this bridge before. He'd never seen anybody within a mile of this spot.

"Hey."

The boy flinched and turned toward him, almost dropping his fishing pole. The boy had a long scar across his right cheek and a bright red sunburn. He wasn't wearing shoes, and his pant cuffs were frayed. His blond hair was shorn closely against his skull.

"Jeez," the boy said. "Where'd you come from?"

Olav hooked his thumb over his shoulder, pointing behind him. The boy looked at the car and scratched beneath the brim of his hat.

"You going to drive over this bridge?"

"No."

The boy nodded.

"Good. It's old. It'll probably break if you try it."

Olav went up to the bridge's railing and peered down into the water. He couldn't tell if the roaring in his head was coming from the river, himself, or both. The boy's fishing line was a long, thin filament that ran from the bridge all the way down to the river below, like a strand of spiderwebbing.

The boy stepped up beside him, and they stared at the river. "Fish ain't bitin' today," the boy said. "Too hot, I guess. They're all stayin' at the bottom of the river where it's cool."

"Huh," Olav said. "Maybe at dusk."

The boy spat off the bridge. He had a lump of tobacco chew tucked into his lower lip. "Don't know if I'd want to be here around dark," he said. "These woods give me the jitters. At first I thought you were a ghost."

"You believe in ghosts?"

The boy spat again over the railing. "Sometimes, I guess."

Olav nodded and rubbed the back of his neck. "Me, too. Actually, I found something that's haunted right now."

The boy snorted and looked at him sideways.

"Sure you did."

Olav held the boy's gaze until his smirk faded.

"It's a skull," Olav said.

"Really?"

"A human skull."

The boy tilted his head, trying to suss Olav out.

"You want to see it? It's in my car."

"Sure."

The boy smiled, his joy wide and simple. Olav led the way across the bridge to the car. He opened the passenger door and pointed at his backpack.

"It's in there."

As the boy came forward to have a look, Olav stepped back and went around to the car's trunk. He popped the trunk's lid, reached inside, and pulled out a crowbar. He returned to the passenger side and found the boy standing beside the car, holding Olav's backpack open with both hands as he peered intently inside it. He looked even younger than eleven now, his mouth hanging slack with amazement.

"Wow, you really did find—"

Olav swung the crowbar evenly, as if he was swinging at a low fastball, and connected solidly with the back of the boy's knees. The boy made a surprised *uhf* sound and pitched against the side of the car, slamming his forehead against the top of the passenger doorway before dropping face-first to the ground. Olav brought the crowbar down two more times, THUMP, THUMP, landing each blow directly on the boy's spine. The boy screamed after the first blow and passed out after the second, his brain shorted out

by the pain. It had been hard to tell over the loud screaming, but Olav was pretty certain he'd heard something
important snap.

The boy had dropped the backpack when he'd fallen,
and the skull had rolled out onto the gravel road. It had
landed upright, facing Olav, and it looked like the rest of
its skeleton body was buried out of sight beneath the gravel.

Olav grabbed the boy by his hair and raised his face
toward the skull.

"How's this?"

Excellent. So young.

"Yeah," Olav said. "That's what I thought."

The boy was surprisingly light. Olav was able to throw
him over his shoulder and carry him back across the bridge.
He dumped him on the bridge's surface and picked up the
boy's fishing pole where he'd left it propped against the railing. Olav reeled in the long fishing line until only two feet
remained and cut the remaining line with his pocket knife.
He cut the scrap of line in half and used one length to tie
the boy's feet together and the other to tie his hands behind
his back. The boy groaned as Olav lifted him off the bridge
by the fishing line knots and swung him back and forth
through the air, one-two-three, and pitched him off the
bridge like a piece of luggage going into the belly of a plane.

Trussed up and lost in his pain, the boy fell silently
through the air and dropped into the river. He bobbed
along the river's surface for a few moments, passing beneath
the bridge and coming into view on the other side, before
the current took him and drew him under. Olav picked out

a metal spinner from the boy's tackle box before chucking both the box and the boy's fishing pole into the river after him.

His work done, Olav wiped his hands on the front of his jeans and exhaled. He felt remarkably calm and reinvigorated, all the confusion he'd been feeling after spending time with Harper Spurling cleared from his mind like a house swept clean. He was ready to go back into town and prepare for the evening. He was ready to party.

The Whirlwind
(1861)

In August 1861, Hawthorn held a dance to celebrate its five-year anniversary, raising a tent big enough to cover the entire town square and constructing a bandstand with wood donated by the Spurling and Helle Lumber Company. The next day, the barometer fell and the summer atmosphere pressed like a vise upon everyone's skulls, making small children prone to tears and the hungover revelers feel even more wretched. Sofie sat with her father at the breakfast table and watched him nurse his coffee while she sketched in her diary. It was Sunday morning, and they'd be going to church soon. Her mother was getting dressed behind the cabin's single curtain, and her sister, Gerta, had gone to fetch fresh water for washing.

"How is your head, Papa?"

Her father rubbed his temple and took a drink of coffee. He sighed.

"It has seen better mornings, I suppose."

"You had too much whiskey last night and now the Devil is taking his toll."

Her father raised his eyebrows.

"The Devil?"

"Mrs. Elsberry says the Devil sits at the bottom of every drink, waiting for you to find him. He smiles with each sip."

Her father shrugged. "Mrs. Elsberry is a fine teacher, Sofie, but I would not call her an enjoyable woman."

Sofie's mother poked her head out from behind the curtain.

"Watch your tongue, Mr. Helle."

"I was only expressing my personal thoughts, Mother."

Sofie grinned. She would need to remember this conversation for the night's diary entry. Mrs. Elsberry was not an enjoyable woman . . .

Gerta burst into the cabin, water sloshing in the bucket she was carrying. She set the bucket down with a heavy splash and pointed out the doorway.

"Papa," Gerta shouted, "come look."

"Papa is feeling poorly from last night's dance," Sofie said, grinning at her sister. "Though I did not see him dance much."

"Lord in heaven," her father said, rising from his chair. "I'll have a look if my family leaves me in peace for a bit."

Sofie put her needlework down and rose as well, curious. She followed her father and her older sister outside the cabin.

"Uff da," her father said. "Such a sky."

"See," Gerta said. "Didn't I tell you?"

Gerta, who was now thirteen to Sofie's eleven, skipped into the yard and danced from one foot to the other. The early afternoon sky had turned a pale gold that matched Sofie's flaxen hair almost perfectly, a color unlike any sky she could remember seeing before. She scanned the horizon in all four directions and found an ugly cloud bank to the far west.

A door slammed. Their neighbor, an old Welshman named Harry Dove, had come outside to see the sky himself. Mr. Dove wore circular, wire-rimmed spectacles and had a wooly, untamable white beard that the neighborhood children loved to grab and pull on until the old man cried uncle. "It's going to blow," Mr. Dove shouted, though he was not a great distance away. "My bad knee's been aching since midnight."

Their father nodded to the old man.

"Ya. I think so, Mr. Dove."

"Those clouds are going to roll over us something fierce before dinnertime," Harry Dove said, laughing and slapping his cheeks. "She'll be a doozy, all right."

Mr. Dove went back into his cabin and slammed his door. Sofie grabbed her older sister's hands and they twirled around in the yard.

"Golden sky, golden sky," they sang, making up one of their little songs.

Their father frowned. "Daughters, I know this weather feels like a lark, but it may turn troublesome. We will go to the Leather Boot and see this storm out in Günter Hahn's cellar."

"Yes, Papa."

Sofie and Gerta stopped spinning and ran inside. They told their mother about the storm and gathered their most important things. Their mother, who always loved a prolonged discussion when it had a chance to rile her husband up, for once agreed immediately and began dropping the family's few valuables into a potato sack. When she was satisfied she'd nabbed everything she could carry, their mother threw the sack over her shoulder and headed out the cabin door without looking back.

"Listen," their father said, walking beside her. "I can carry that sack, Mother."

"You worry about yourself, Papa," their mother said, elbowing him off. "I'll see to my silver, thank you."

They crossed the river and found Günter Hahn standing outside his tavern, watching the sky with Tárlach Brodigan, Daniel Spurling, and Eldon Hawthorn. "*Ser gut,*" Mr. Hahn called out. "The old camp is now here together."

Ilsa Hahn, Günter Hahn's wife, appeared in the doorway and held out her arms. Sighing as if she'd carried the stuffed sack across three tall mountains, their mother handed it over to the German. Mrs. Hahn nodded curtly at Sofie's father and went inside the tavern with their mother and Gerta. Sofie lingered outside, not yet ready to leave the exciting scene. Her father shook hands with the other men as if the storm were a meeting he'd called personally. He cocked his eyebrow and grinned as he shook Mr. Hawthorn's hand.

"The new Mrs. Hawthorn agreed to visit a pub? I thought she had strict rules about dens of iniquity."

"I have lost one wife," Mr. Hawthorn replied, looking grim. "I am not going to lose another."

The men turned to the approaching storm. The sky was still a peculiar gold, and the clouds to the west had grown larger and darker. Even as they watched, the storm front came on fast and whipped the high prairie grass. An old woman ran through the street, holding a cat to her chest and clutching her bonnet with her free hand. The men murmured among themselves, wondering if she wanted assistance, but in another moment a cabin door was flung open and she sprinted inside, slamming the door shut behind her. Sofie wondered if the old woman had lost her mind.

Mr. Spurling spat tobacco on the ground. "How many folks have root cellars, you reckon?"

"Not so many," Mr. Hahn said. "But my little tavern cellar is already filled, like the ark before the flood."

The wind worsened to a howl, and the cloud bank neared. It was now a tremendous black wall, higher than anything made by man. As it rolled in, it cast a shadow over the town and blotted out the straw yellow sky. They would need to go inside soon.

"There is something of the Lord in this storm, I'm thinking," Mr. Brodigan said, removing his cap and holding it in his hands.

"The Lord is in all things," Mr. Hawthorn said, still watching the sky.

"Aye. Yet maybe there is a little more of the Lord in this."

Sofie's father rubbed his cheek.

"The Lord or the Devil. Sometimes there is no telling."

They took refuge in the tavern's cellar as the wind howled above them. With Mr. Hahn's friends, family, and all the whiskey barrels, the cellar was packed so tightly you could taste what your neighbors had eaten for breakfast with each inhalation of breath. Sofie was crammed into a corner and surrounded by her family. She would have preferred to sit on the floor, but it was too crowded even to do that.

"You might have gotten rid of the liquor," the second Mrs. Hawthorn said, angling her head to get a look at Mr. Hahn. "It might have improved our comfort a good deal."

"Are you mad, woman?" Mr. Brodigan said, shouting above the wind. "We will be needing all this whiskey after the storm passes."

Sofie leaned against her father's side. The noise above rose to yet another level, the sound of wood splintering joining the general howling above their heads. She pictured Death in his hooded black cloak, high above the earth and looking down at all the living as if they were nothing but ants to be stepped upon.

The roof above them began to groan. Sofie trembled, her heart beating with an amazing rapidity. A board cracked and pulled away from the ceiling, sucked into the churning darkness above. Sofie closed her eyes. Another board cracked, and another. A woman screamed, and the wind finally found them, pouring into the cellar and buffeting them all.

Sofie felt herself growing lighter.

And lighter.

She opened her eyes. Though it was midday, the patch

of sky she could see through the few remaining ceiling boards was utterly black, without a crack of light. Sofie realized it wasn't Death up above the town, but God. That darkness was what God looked like when He made His presence felt upon the world.

Sofie closed her eyes again, fighting against the wind's upward pull. She knew they would survive this whirlwind, that the fierce wind would stop blowing soon enough, but she still wished she'd kept her eyes shut. She felt certain she had seen something she should not have. A secret that did not belong to the living.

13

AFTER OLAV DROPPED her off, Harper was surprised to find her house empty and quiet. She found a note from her mother saying they'd gone to pick up Grandma Spurling. Tonight was family grill-out night, which meant The Dad would grill in the backyard and they'd all stuff their faces until they could barely move. Harper checked the refrigerator and discovered coleslaw, potato salad, and a dozen ears of sweet corn waiting to be shucked. She poured herself a glass of water and went downstairs to her bedroom, which was pleasantly cool. She opened the curtains, flooding the room with sunlight, and sat down at her desk. She thumbed a text to Eva, who, of course, texted her back in less than five seconds.

> Guess what? I've got a date for the party tonight
>
> NO FUCKING WAY!!! WHO?

Harper smiled and counted to three.

> WHO IS IT HARPER TELL ME RIGHT THE FUCK NOW
>   LADY
>
> Jesus chill out it's Olav Helle
>
> ROADKILL BOY?!?!
>
> Don't call him that):
>
> SORRY!
>
> And stop using all CAPS
>
> Ahhh! Harper Spurling has a boyfriend!!!

Settle down. He's just giving me a ride to the party, that's all.

OMG that's my job! Bastard!

Harper laughed.

See ya later

Okay shave your legs!

Blerg.

DO IT!

Byeeee

Harper set her phone down on the desk and picked up Sofie Helle's diary.

May 19th, 1862
Dear Diary,

Spring rains again today but not every minute. Gerta and I went for a walk during one of the halts in the storming and picked wildflowers for Mama. I gathered a big bouquet of purple thistles with sprigs of green and tied it together with a piece of twine I found in the bottom of the sewing chest.

While we were picking flowers the storm clouds rumbled over the mountains in the distance. It sounded like the whole sky would crack apart, like Gabriel blowing his horn. When it started to rain again we laughed and raced back to the cabin. I won like always!

Yours,
Sofie

Harper flipped to the back of the book. The entries got kind of weird at the end, and then they stopped altogether. Mrs. Randolph had said there was no record of what Sofie Helle had grown up to do or how she'd died. Sofie's adult life was a pure mystery.

July 22nd, 1866
Dear Diary,

This has been the hottest summer I can remember. Gerta and I go swimming every afternoon. The current is getting lazier the longer summer continues, though once in a while if I am not paying attention I feel a strong undertow that tugs at my feet. Sometimes we float down the river holding onto logs, our faces upturned to the sky. The sunlight surges into me and when I close my eyes I can almost imagine I am in Heaven.

Then we wash ashore in the crook of the river, walk back up the riverbank, and float all the way down again.

Yours,
    Sofie

July 23rd, 1866
Dear Diary,

The weather is still hot. This afternoon I felt a deep current in the river that felt so cold it was as if I'd stepped into a bucket of snow. Strange how the river can feel so warm on top and so cold at the bottom.

Gerta thinks I'm imagining the coldness in the river though Papa says it's possible. He says rivers have secret lives of their own, just like beasts in the forest.

Yours,
    Sofie

The final diary entry was the strangest of all.

July 24th, 1866
Dear Diary,

Today was hot again. I have been dreaming about all the buffalo that have been killed on the plains by buffalo hunters. I saw a picture in the newspaper of a wide field filled with their bones. It looked like a graveyard for giants. They say many buffalo are slaughtered for sport and only their wooly skins are harvested while the meat is left to rot in the sun. The smell must be terrible and I can only imagine the clouds of flies buzzing in the air.

Yours,
    Sofie

Dead buffalo dreams? Ending the whole diary? What the hell? Harper turned back to the diary's first page and started reading the whole thing over again.

———

Everyone came home, and they started making dinner. Harper helped in the kitchen, hoping to speed the whole process along. After exchanging cell phone numbers, Olav had said he'd pick her up at 7:30 for the party at Kira Fredrickson's cabin. For cover, Harper was going to tell her parents she was going to her friend Tina Hoegaard's house. No way would The Mom let her go to an unsupervised party out at some cabin in the mountains.

"So I'm going to hang out at Tina's tonight," Harper said to her mother as they stood side by side at the sink, shucking sweet corn while the kettle of water heated up on the stove. Grandma Spurling sat at the kitchen table, reading an issue of *Cosmo* and drinking non-doctor-approved white wine. "We're going to have a movie marathon."

"Tina Hoegaard?" The Mom said, turning her powerful Momdar on Harper. "You haven't talked about her for a while. I thought you weren't friends anymore."

"We're still friends. What's there to talk about all the time?"

"I don't know. Didn't you have a fight?"

"That was last year, Mom. We're over it."

The Mom grinned.

"Ahhh. I get it. Everybody else is busy and you're scraping the bottom of the friend barrel, huh?"

The Mom glanced at Grandma Spurling, who was absorbed in her magazine.

"All right," The Mom said. "Be home by ten."

"That's in less than three hours. It's a movie marathon, not a movie quickie."

"I always liked quickies," Grandma Spurling said, looking up. "Ten minutes of rolling around, a little cleanup, then you can get on with your day."

"Gross, Grandma. Gross."

"What? You don't think I ever used seven ways to please my man?"

"Mom, please," The Mom said.

"You two had the birds and the bees talk already, right?"

"Yes, Mom. That was five years ago."

Grandma Spurling smiled and took a sip of wine. "Goodness, I wish I'd been invited to that chat."

"It really wasn't that exciting, Grandma," Harper said. "We have the Internet these days, you know."

The Mom rolled her eyes. The water had started to boil on the stove.

"Fine. Be home by midnight, and get Tina to drive you home."

"She only lives eight blocks away."

"Deal or no deal?"

"Fine. Deal."

And that was it for the interrogation. Pretty mild for The Mom. Maybe she was losing her edge, or she was just so sick of everybody being in the house since school ended she didn't mind some mild shenanigans. Harper took the plate of shucked sweet corn over to the stove and added the ears to the kettle one at a time. The Mom left the kitchen to bring plates outside to the patio table and check on the grilling. The only sound in the kitchen was the water boiling and the distant buzz of somebody in the neighborhood mowing a lawn. Harper could feel her grandmother's gaze scanning her from across the kitchen. The sensation was very similar to Momdar.

"You're sneaking off to a party, aren't you, sweetie?"

Harper turned her head.

"What?"

"Oh, you've got that devious glow. Don't worry. I won't tell."

"Grandma—"

"Just promise me you'll be safe, okay?"

Harper sighed and looked down at the kitchen floor. Just once she wanted to get away with something.

"Okay, I promise."

"Good kiddo," Grandma Spurling said, taking another drink of wine. "A girl can never be too careful."

14

BY 7:30 HARPER had escaped her family's clutches and was walking toward Tina Hoegaard's house with her purse slung over her shoulder and a fresh, going-to-a-party-without-looking-too-obvious-about-it outfit on. She'd texted Tina's address to Olav, and he was waiting for her as she came up the sidewalk, his car idling with the windows rolled up.

Harper wondered for a moment with the small, dippy rom-com part of her brain if Olav was going to get out and open the passenger door for her, but he stayed in the driver's seat and stared straight ahead, zoning out. She opened the passenger door herself and slid in, looking back at the Hoegaards' house as she slammed the door, wondering if Tina or Mrs. Hoegaard had spotted her. She should have chosen a pickup spot a block farther up, she realized, but it was too late for smartness now.

"Hey," she said, buckling her seat belt and setting her purse on the floor.

"Hey."

Olav put the car in drive and they started down the street.

"Thanks for picking me up."

Olav was dressed exactly as he had been earlier that day. Boys.

"So you know how to get to Mount Pale, right?"

"Yeah."

"So drive that way and I'll tell you when to turn off."

"Okay."

They drove through town and turned left onto the highway, headed south. The sun was getting lower in the west but was still high enough that its orange light flooded the car and made Harper whip her sun visor to the side, which sort of helped. The sunlight made the mountains turn orange and pinkish, and it seemed as if they were driving on an alien planet, maybe Mars but with a ton of pine trees. Harper sighed and sank back into the car seat, happy.

Olav glanced in the rearview mirror. Harper wondered what his deal was. His real deal.

"Your parents don't care if you go to a party in the mountains?"

"They didn't ask," Olav said. "They don't really notice what I do. I go out a lot at night."

"Right. Delivering pizzas to hungry pizza eaters."

Olav looked at her. "I like to go on walks, too."

"Even though you have a car?"

"Yeah."

"You're a thinker," Harper said. "Like Socrates."

Olav grinned and the corner of his mouth hooked in a sexy way. Harper's phone vibrated in her pocket, startling her. It was Eva, wondering if she was still coming to the party. Harper texted back Yes we are and turned her phone to no vibrate or ring.

"Do you go to a lot of parties?"

Olav shook his head. "No. This is my first one."

"Me too. I mean, it's my first kegger."

Olav didn't say anything. The car was quiet except for the sound of the engine and the tires on the road. Harper turned the radio on and winced at the static. She hit the six presets but they were all set to non-channels. She had to scan to find a real station.

"Don't you listen to the radio?"

"No," Olav said. "I don't like it."

"Oh."

Harper flicked the radio off and sat back. They rode in silence into the mountains, the Clawhooks watching them on their maybe-date.

———

Kira Fredrickson's cabin had a hot tub in the backyard Harper didn't remember from the summer before. Kira's parents worked for a natural gas company and made tons of money. They always let Kira do pretty much whatever she wanted, like having keggers at the family cabin with no adults around. Harper hadn't brought a swimsuit, but Kira had an extra and Harper changed into it in the cabin's bathroom. When she went back outside, the sun had set and everybody was either sitting around a campfire or in the hot tub. Harper scanned the crowd and saw Olav already sitting in the hot tub with his shirt off and a cup of beer in his hand. Eva was in the tub, too, along with Kira Fredrickson, Kira's boyfriend, Josh Keegan, and Tony Sooner. Eva had been dating Tony for a couple of weeks, and she said she liked him even though he was as dumb as a rock. Harper approached the hot tub, feeling awkward and shy as she climbed the tub's wooden steps. Kira's swimsuit was a little tight on her.

"Harper Spurling!" Eva shouted, already sounding drunk. "Get in here, sexy!"

Harper dipped a foot into the tub and winced. The water felt like it'd been boiling under the sun all day.

"Don't worry," Kira said, smiling. "You get used to it."

Harper got in farther and sat down, gasping as the heat washed over her.

Used to it.

Right.

She stood up and swung around in Olav's direction, sitting in the empty spot beside him on the tub's edge. Everybody had left room around him, she realized. Knowing that his date was in the cabin, changing. Eva the horny wing-girl had probably given the group an order.

Olav grabbed a plastic cup from the hot tub's ledge and offered it to her.

"I got you a beer."

"Cool. Thanks."

Harper leaned back and kicked her legs up, letting the bubbling water float her. The water was growing tolerable, and the hot tub had a great view of the plain below. Harper sipped the beer, which tasted like beer, and contemplated the sunset to the west and Hawthorn to the north. She lived down there, in that tiny city. Every day she lived down there, with her tiny friends and her tiny family, and went to her tiny school. She'd be a junior in the fall. Soon she'd be getting ready to go to college and live somewhere far, far away. You could basically see her whole sixteen years of life from up here.

"This is cool," Olav said, leaning his head back against the hot tub's rim and floating beside her. He'd set down his beer, and she could see his bare chest rising above the water. It looked as smooth as a girl's. "I've never been in a hot tub before."

"What?" Harper said. "Really?"

"Yeah."

"Not even in a hotel on vacation?"

"My family doesn't go on vacations much. At least, not hotel vacations. We usually go camping."

Harper turned onto her side so she could look at him more closely. "Yeah," she said, "my parents aren't big campers. My dad says sleeping on the ground is an insult to the homeless."

"Well, he's missing out. The woods are great."

"What about the bugs and the poison ivy? And no showers?"

Olav drifted in the water and gently bumped against her side, sending an electric tremble through Harper. "That's all part of it," Olav said. "You get used to the bugs and being dirty after a couple of days, and it doesn't bother you so much."

Harper tried to imagine her family camping in a tent together for a whole week in the middle of nowhere. No electricity, no toilets. Like Sofie Helle must have lived all the way from Missouri to Hawthorn, covering ten miles a day while staring at oxen butt.

"You find cool things in the woods, too."

"Yeah? Like what?"

Olav turned onto his side, facing her. Their faces were close to touching.

"You can't tell anybody."

"I won't."

"You swear?"

Harper raised her hand above the water and offered her pinky. Olav stared at it for a second before hooking it with his own.

Even this stupid little pinkie swear made Harper shiver, God help her.

15

OLAV HESITATED A second, thinking. Telling Harper wouldn't be the same thing as showing the skull to the boy he'd thrown into the river earlier that afternoon. He wasn't going to kill Harper Spurling. He just wanted to kiss her before the night was over.

"I found a skull," Olav said, and it felt good to tell her. He was tired of keeping so many secrets. So many cool and interesting secrets that were way better than any of the secrets these other boring rich kids were hiding. Who cared how drunk they got at parties or if they tried cocaine once or if they gave each other blow jobs while driving? That was nothing. That was kid stuff. They didn't know anything about death or love or what it felt like to drop a human being into the river and watch him wash away.

Harper's eyes widened.

"A human skull?"

"Yep. Except its lower jaw. That's missing."

"Holy shit."

Harper pulled herself onto the tub's ledge and sat back, dangling her feet into the bubbling water. Olav sat up on the tub's ledge but remained below the waterline, pushing his growing erection down with the palm of his hand. Everybody else in the hot tub had coupled up and were snuggling and kissing. This was a make-out party, he realized. The kind they talked about at school. Make-out parties actually existed.

"How'd you find it?" Harper asked, slowly kicking her feet back and forth in the water. "Just walking around in the woods like Davy Crockett?"

Olav drank the rest of his beer and burped.

"No. I dug it up."

"So you go around randomly digging in the woods?"

"I was burying a cat."

Harper laughed.

"A cat?"

"My neighbor's cat. It died and I said I'd bury it for them."

"How'd it die?"

Olav tossed his empty cup over the side of the hot tub. The campfire crowd was laughing on the other side of the cabin's yard. A guy was playing a guitar.

"Their dad ran it over when he was backing out of the driveway. I guess it fell asleep under his truck."

"Jeez. Poor kitty."

"Yeah," Olav said, remembering Cooper. Fat and friendly, the tabby cat always liked the roadkill smell coming from their front porch. If you started petting him, he'd roll over right away and show you his belly, like a dog.

"So you were digging a hole for the cat and you found a skull instead? That must have been freaky."

"I took it inside and soaked it in bleach. I thought it would turn white, but it stayed this brownish-yellow."

"It must be really old. You should show it to a scientist."

"I don't know any scientists."

"What about Mr. Zegans? He teaches science. You could ask him about it."

Olav nodded.

"Maybe."

Harper adjusted her bikini top. Olav looked up at the stars and did his best to ignore the kissing shadows around him. He still had no idea how he'd ended up driving Harper Spurling to a party, much less telling her about the skull. This was a strange day. It seemed as if it had been going on forever.

Harper slid back under the water onto the ledge beside him. Olav looked up and realized the sun had gone down a while ago. The night sky was on fire with stars.

"Hey," Harper said, leaning toward him. "Do you want to kiss me?"

Kiss her.

Olav flinched.

Then take her to the river.

He stood up in the hot tub and looked around, forgetting about his hard-on. It was the skull. Somehow it had traveled here.

One more kill. That's all the stars require.

"Olav? Hellooo?"

Where are you? Olav thought.

I am in the sky tonight. I am on the wind.

Harper grabbed his hand and squeezed it.

"You okay?"

Olav looked down, bewildered, and saw that Harper Spurling was still holding his hand, looking freaked out.

"Sorry," he said, his mind buzzing. "I think we should go back."

"What?"

"Yeah," Olav said, pulling his hand away. "Sorry."

———————

Olav knew he'd made a mistake with Harper. As they drove back to town, she was quiet and lay slumped against the passenger window. He should have kept his trap shut. He should have ignored what the skull was saying and kept hanging out. Shit. He was always fucking up somehow. Like with Cooper. Why hadn't he checked under the car before he'd pulled out of the driveway? He knew the stupid cat liked to sleep under there.

Though what was one more dead cat in the world? Olav had scraped up dozens off the county highways with his father. Maybe a hundred. They died like every other animal in the world. Including humans. Humans died the same as cats and skunks and deer, and none of it meant anything, not even the pain they felt before they died.

That got lost, too.

Everything got lost.

"What are you thinking about?"

Harper was watching him from her corner, her face blue in the dashboard light. She could have been a ghost. A dead hitchhiker he'd mistakenly picked up along the road.

"Nothing," Olav said, refocusing on the road.

Harper sat up.

"Come on. Tell me."

They passed a dead possum that lay curled in upon itself on the side of the road. You didn't see many possums around. He'd have to tell Dad.

"Do you ever think about death?" Olav asked, glancing at Harper.

"Sure," Harper said, leaning her head back against her seat. "I think about Sofie and how she's been dead, like, for a hundred years, probably. It's weird reading somebody's diary and knowing they're dead."

"I guess so. I never really cared about her."

"Really? And she's your own relative?"

Olav shrugged. "I never met her. I just read her diary like everybody else."

"You need to meet somebody to care about them?"

"I guess so."

"That's kind of messed up."

Olav didn't say anything. He'd never talked about any of this before. Not even with the skull.

"You were just thinking about that skull you dug up, weren't you?" Harper said. "That's why you asked me about death."

Olav stared at Harper, wondering for a second if she could read his mind the same way the skull did. He thought *I want to have sex with you doggy style* to see if she flinched.

She didn't.

Olav turned his gaze back on the road. They'd entered the Hawthorn city limits. They'd be at her house soon.

"I think death is all around us," Olav said. "I mean, it's kind of like air. Actually, death is in the air, too. Things had to die to make air and to make us and to make everything else. We're living on death. And death's living on us. Really living on us. Like, we have to feed it, or else it starves, and that throws the world off balance."

"Right. Have you seen the news lately? I think death's eating pretty good."

"That's because humans are so good at helping it. We're the best killers in the history of the earth."

Olav slowed the car as they turned off onto a smaller residential street.

"So you think humans evolved . . . because death wanted extra help?"

"Maybe." Olav shrugged. "Maybe death got greedy."

Harper shook her head. "Death is a naturally occurring force in the universe. It doesn't have a consciousness. It doesn't feel greed or lust or jealousy. It's not human."

"Maybe not. But it can take human form."

"Like the Grim Reaper?"

Olav nodded. "Exactly."

They pulled up in front of the Spurlings' house, and Olav put the car in park without turning off the engine. Harper unbuckled her seat belt and popped her door open, which turned on the car's dome light.

"Thanks for the ride."

Olav nodded, gripping the steering wheel with both hands and clenching his jaw. Why did she make him so nervous? He was bigger than she was. He could strangle her with his bare hands if he wanted to.

"See ya," Harper said. She watched him for another moment, as if waiting for something. Olav had no idea what to do or say, so he kept his mouth shut. "Well, good luck with that skull," Harper said at last, breaking the awkward silence.

"Thanks," Olav said. Harper slipped out of the car and slammed the door behind her, already halfway up her front walk before Olav could put the car in drive. He pictured Harper in Kira's swimsuit, asking if he wanted to kiss her, and wondered if he should be feeling what people called regret. He pulled away from the Spurlings' house with a loud engine rev and sped through their neighborhood, blowing through every stop sign on his way home.

Olav had told Harper the truth about how he felt, but not all of it. He didn't really care about people he'd met in person, either. Not his mother or his father or even himself. When he looked in the mirror, he didn't see anything that much different from a dead fox or a dead raccoon. Not really. Since he'd dug up the skull the previous November, Olav had come to believe he was just in a different state of being—a currently not-dead state—that allowed him to do what he wanted in *this* reality until his heart gave out and his lungs stopped working and he moved on to the *next* reality. He was actually just a ghost on vacation from death.

And ghosts didn't care about the living, did they?

No.

They just kept haunting until they were satisfied.

The Outlaw
(1863)

Hawthorn was rebuilt nearly from scratch after the fearsome windstorm of 1861, which claimed forty-seven lives and clogged the Tender Heart River with drowned livestock. On a Sunday afternoon in June 1863, Sofie Helle was out walking around town, relishing the fine summer day. Now that Sofie was thirteen years old, she had begun to find her entire family irritating (especially her older sister, Gerta), and she'd taken to going on long walks to enjoy periods of quiet and the peace of her own thoughts. She brought her diary with her when she went on these constitutionals, carrying it in a leather pouch that hung from her shoulder by a slender rawhide strap. She could be seen all about town, sitting in contemplation while she wrote, her brow creased as she gnawed at the end of her pencil.

Sofie was walking past her father's sawmill, which was closed for the Lord's Day, when she heard a loud clattering and a man cursing. The entrance door to the mill had been forced open and was slightly ajar. Sofie, who'd been looking for a worthy adventure, found her interest piqued. She slipped inside the factory and paused to allow her eyes to adjust to the dim light. She reckoned it would be a mill worker fooling around, perhaps lifting a few tools for private use, but as her eyes adjusted she was surprised to see a stranger picking through a tool bench, tossing aside chisels and handsaws as he stood absorbed in his search. The stranger swayed slightly on his feet.

"What are you doing in here?"

The stranger straightened.

"Why?" he said, without turning around. "You going to tattle on me, girl?"

Sofie frowned.

"I haven't decided one way or another yet. Why don't you leave my papa's tools be? They aren't yours."

"I am looking for tongs of some kind. Something for picking."

"Picking what?"

The stranger turned and grinned at Sofie, showing his black teeth and a handsome, heavily weathered face. He had gray eyes, a large nose that appeared to have been broken many times, and a wide, proud jaw. He flapped his left shoulder and she could see his shirt was soaked with blood.

"I'd like to pick out a bullet."

"You've been shot?"

"Yes, Miss. Ain't the first time, either."

"You must not be a farmer."

The stranger laughed and picked up a chisel. "Clever girl. Mayhap I can pry the bullet out with this here picker?"

"Use that tool and your arm will get infected. You'll wake up tomorrow with a greater problem than you have now."

The stranger sighed and tossed the chisel down.

"Ain't that the way it always is."

Sofie noted the stranger wore a pistol strapped to his

hip in a leather holster, just like a dime novel gunfighter. She had never seen a man wearing a gun like that in true life. Even Hawthorn's sheriff generally went about unarmed, pulling out his scattergun only on Saturday nights when he made a friendly tour of the taverns.

"Where are you visiting us from, sir?"

"I come recently out of the wilderness," the stranger said, picking up pliers. "Where man is beast and beast is man."

Sofie wondered if the stranger meant to kill her. The idea electrified her skin like a cool, unexpected touch.

"I'll tend to your arm," Sofie said, stepping forward. "Find a chair to sit on and a block of wood to bite. There's a doctoring kit in my father's office meant for the mill workers. I'm not bad with a needle and thread, and Lord knows I've seen my mother stitch up enough men."

The stranger turned on his heel and smiled his rotten smile.

"Why, girl, how mighty Christian of you."

———————

The stranger's name was Crack Donegan. Donegan declared he was a hardened outlaw who'd run into a patch of hard luck but wouldn't delve into the specific acts of lawlessness he'd committed due, he claimed, to a distaste for braggery and self-aggrandizement. Sofie sterilized the pliers and a fine chisel, dug around in the meat of the outlaw's left arm, and managed to finally extract the bullet. Donegan chatted the entire time, despite the obvious pain the rough surgery was causing him. By the time Sofie had sewn up Donegan's wound and bandaged it, she found herself liking the outlaw despite the heady aura of danger and mayhem he gave off. Here was a rough soul with a gleam in his eye you never saw in town folk, who'd grown soft and comfortable with a carpentered life.

Donegan flapped his arm and considered the fresh bandage. "Goddamn if she doesn't ache like you ripped the bones right out."

"You'll need to rest it a few days to let it properly heal."

"Shoot. I can't recall a time when one part of me or another wasn't busy healing." Donegan winked slyly at Sofie. "Course, laying low for a spell wouldn't hurt anything. Not all the folks I have encountered recently have acted as high Christian as yourself."

"I feel as if I shouldn't know anything about that."

Donegan raised his chin and looked over Sofie's shoulder, staring off with an unfocused gaze. "I wish I didn't know anything about it either. Mayhap then I could sleep sounder at night."

Sofie cleaned her makeshift surgical tools with a rag and studied the outlaw. The factory had fallen into a deep Sunday quiet, with sunlight streaming in rows through the high windows all around. It reminded her of church before the Sunday crowd arrived. She brought the tools over to the bench and set them down, turning her back on the outlaw for the first time.

"You could camp out in the woods," she said. "I know a few spots where you'd go unnoticed and heal comfortably."

"I have a horse tied up outside. He is in even worse shape than I."

"You could bring the horse as well. There's a logging road that goes for several miles into the forest. My papa's company owns it."

"Ah," Donegan said. "I thought you smelled like pine sap."

Sofie turned back around. She half expected the outlaw to have the pistol leveled at her, followed by a command to empty her pockets and lie down, but Crack Donegan was still slumped in his chair, legs splayed out. He wore black cowboy boots, sharp-toed and worn in the heel. His coat and pants were tattered and dotted with holes.

"So a campout, then," the outlaw said, springing to his feet with a stunning rapidity. "Lead the way, Good Samaritan."

They left the mill's dusty interior and went out into the lumberyard. The outlaw's horse turned out to be a spiny, headstrong creature. Donegan led it by the bridle through town while Sofie followed a hundred yards behind. After they passed through the final ring of houses—all stiff and new—Donegan paused, and Sofie caught up with the outlaw and his unpleasant horse. She pointed the way to the logging road, and they soon turned down it, pine trees encroaching upon them on both sides as they slowly descended into the valley east of town.

"By Charlie, this is a spooky wood," Donegan said, eyeing the shadowed trees. "It has a watching feel to it."

"Yes," Sofie said, nodding, "it does."

Donegan's horse whinnied and whipped its head about. Donegan stroked its neck and cooed to it.

"Your folks settled near these woods on purpose? They must have more sand than most."

"No," Sofie said, shaking her head. "We'd been run here by wolves and didn't have a better option."

"Ah," Donegan said. "I know how that goes."

A full-grown buck sprang onto the logging road thirty feet ahead of them, a dark blur of antlers and fur sprinting for the road's other side. Donegan drew his pistol in one fluid motion and fired, dropping the buck before the animal could dive back into cover. When they walked up to the buck, it was bleeding out onto the grass with a hole in its neck. Donegan holstered his gun and grabbed the buck by its antlers, snapping its neck in one strong twist.

"He'll make a fine fry-up tonight, eh?"

"I'll say," Sofie said, shaking her head. "That was some shot."

The outlaw winked at her.

"They don't call me Crack for nothing."

———

Sofie left the outlaw and his spiny horse as they made camp east of town on the edge of the valley. She walked briskly back to town, wondering exactly what she'd gotten herself involved in, and she had dinner with her family as if it were any other Sunday evening in July. She slept fitfully that night and woke earlier than normal the next morning, gathering some old clothes along with bread and cheese and taking them into the forest on horseback. She returned to the clearing on the edge of the valley and left her horse on the logging road, tied to a tree. Crack Donegan was already awake and perched before a crackling fire, warming his hands as he rocked on his heels.

"My Samaritan," the outlaw called out. "Good morning."

Sofie pushed through the scrub and entered the clearing, carrying the clothes and provisions as if they were a bundle of wood.

"My name is Sofie. How does the day find you?"

The outlaw stood up from his fire, eyeing the clothes. He looked pale and hollow around the eyes. "I have been better, to be honest. The trees rattled all night, and when I woke this morning I found my horse no longer in camp, with no trace to mark its departure."

Sofie halted midway across the clearing.

"You didn't hobble it?"

"That's the curious part. I did indeed. I remember doing so as clear as day."

"Truly?"

"Aye."

"It must have been thieves, then."

"No," Donegan said, spitting on the ground. "I wasn't drunk, and no man can sneak on me without alcohol in my belly. Besides, what thief would come strolling through this deep wood and feel satisfied by stealing one scrawny horse?"

Sofie frowned. The problem was beyond her. No one stole anything in Hawthorn besides the occasional sweet.

"What's that you're carrying, anyhow? A newborn babe?"

Sofie crossed the clearing and deposited her burden in the outlaw's arms. The outlaw set the bundle on the ground and unwrapped it. He picked up the bread and cheese and hefted them in his hands.

"Thank you, Miss Sofie. You are a fine Weegie."

Sofie scowled at the name-calling and looked at the fire.

"Good thing, this bread," Donegan said. "That deer I shot yesterday was no good."

Sofie looked back at the outlaw, her eyebrows angling together.

"What do you mean?"

"Meat was sour," Donegan said, biting into the cheese. "Hurt my stomach until I couldn't force another bite down, though I've been hungry as tarnation. Never tasted the like before."

Sofie came round the fire to get a better look at the outlaw's arm. The bandage was still wrapped tightly, though blood had seeped through the material and dried.

"How is your wound healing?"

Donegan lifted his arm and winced. "I'd be lying if I said it didn't ache something fierce. I dreamt I'd rolled over and fell into my campfire." Donegan started to laugh, but the noise caught in his throat and died out.

"Can you hold out another night here? I have a spare horse I can bring you tomorrow morning. I need to go back into town or else they will start hunting for me."

Donegan ripped off another hunk of bread. He chewed slowly, looking past Sofie and into the trees. "Honestly, Miss, I do not know if I can hold out. This wood is like nothing I have seen before. I believe God may have abandoned this place. Mayhap this whole area."

"So you'll leave today? On foot?"

Donegan turned his gaze from the trees onto Sofie. His eyes were exceptionally bright, as if he had a high fever.

"I don't know. By what fleet means did you arrive at my camp so early in this fine dewy morning? By horse, I suspect?"

Sofie held the outlaw's gaze, unflinching. Her father always said you never turned your back on a wild animal lest you wanted to be its dinner.

"Aye," Donegan said finally, his eyes going flat. "I can wait till tomorrow. Mayhap I can shoot tastier game for tonight's dinner."

"Yes. Hopefully."

The outlaw wrapped up the bread and cheese and rubbed his hands over the fire, sending crumbs into the flames.

"Do you believe in Hell, Miss?"

Sofie considered the question.

"Yes, I suppose I do."

"And do you think it lies deep inside the earth?"

"That I cannot say."

The outlaw nodded, as if he'd expected this response. "Well, I believe it must be inside the earth itself. Yes, sir. I think Hell is what keeps the world weighted down and all of us poor sinners from sailing into the air. Like an anchor."

The outlaw spat into the fire.

"You know, Miss, I heard a story about this area once."

"Oh?"

"I was hunting game with an old Cheyenne pal of mine. He knew more stories than the Bible holds, I reckon. He told me that somewhere around those yonder southern mountains an old tribe once lived."

"Sioux? Apaches?"

Donegan shook his head. "No, that was the twist of it. He said they weren't Indians like we know 'em. He said they was born only a week after the sky spirits and they were all medicine men, the whole lot of them, including the women. He called them The Ones Who Built in Darkness. He said they could send their spirits out at will and influence animals and people. Run them like puppets, if you get my meaning. They could even send their spirits into the stars like cannon shot."

Sofie looked up at the patch of sky above the clearing, trying to picture what a spirit would look like as it soared through the sky.

"But their magic had a steep cost, you see. They needed to take lives to feed it. The Ones Who Built in Darkness needed blood; human if they could get it. My pal said they ended up killing everything in sight and finally turned on each other. They wiped themselves out instead of giving up their magic."

"My goodness," Sofie said, placing her hand over her heart.

"Yes, Miss. Isn't that a fine story for a young girl's ears?"

———————

Sofie rode out to Crack Donegan's camp once again early the next morning. She brought more provisions, the promised horse, and a shovel for burying the outlaw's campfire. She left the horses tied up on the logging road and set the shovel upon her shoulder. She noticed the woods were unusually quiet. All the morning songbirds and normally piping insects were mute. As she entered the clearing, she saw Donegan's campfire had burnt down yet was still smoldering, a wisp of smoke rising above it like a snake curling into the air.

Sofie called hello but received no answer. A few yards from the fire, amid the bundle of clothes Sofie had brought the day before, she found Crack Donegan lying face up on the ground, his narrow boots pointed to the sky. He was dead, his gray eyes still open to the world. He had a dark hole in his right temple and was holding his pistol in his right hand. The air still smelled like gunpowder.

A scrap of paper was tucked into the collar of Donegan's shirt. Sofie bent down and retrieved the scrap. The script was large and blocky, like a child's, and only one line:

O I seen the Long Night and it was not for me

Sofie folded the scrap of paper carefully and put it in her pocket. She searched the clearing for a suitable gravesite, telling herself that she hadn't truly brought the shovel for this purpose—that when she'd woken earlier that morning in the lonesome predawn darkness, wondering if she'd heard something like a shot in the distance, she'd fully believed she would find a living, jesting man at this campsite.

Sofie picked a flat spot of ground and set to digging with a heavy heart, already figuring the evening's diary entry in her mind.

It wasn't every day you buried an outlaw.

16

THE NIGHT OF Kira Fredrickson's hot tub party, Harper dreamed Sofie Helle was leading her through Hawthorn on a cold, foggy day, keeping her distance as Harper followed about ten yards behind, never able to totally catch up with her. They'd gone on and on for miles, down streets Harper thought looked familiar but didn't exactly recognize, until they came to a dark thundercloud that was as high as a skyscraper. Sofie glanced back at Harper, her face solemn and pale, before walking into the cloud and disappearing from sight.

Then Harper woke up, covered in sweat though her basement bedroom was freezing cold. Her clock radio said it was only 6:12.

Harper groaned and pulled the covers over her head.

No, no, no.

Too early. She needed to go back to sleep.

Sleeeeeeep.

But . . . nope.

Harper threw back the covers. The sun was already rising outside, illuminating the edges of her curtains. She opened the curtains fully and picked her way through the pile of clothes on the floor, digging out her running shorts, tennis shoes, and the athletic armband she wore to listen to music on her cell phone. She got dressed quickly, trembling in the room's air-conditioned overkill, and went upstairs to use the bathroom. The house was quiet and dark. When Harper came out of the bathroom, The Mom was standing in the living room and looking out the front window. Her blond hair was messy from sleep, and she was wearing her ratty old pink bathrobe. "You're up early," she said, looking back at Harper.

"Yeah."

"Going for a run?"

"Might as well."

"You sleep okay?"

Harper shrugged. She didn't really feel like talking about Sofie Helle with The Mom. Sofie was her thing, not The Mom's.

"Well, a run will do you good," The Mom said. "I should join you sometime."

Harper raised her eyebrows at the thought.

"Hey, I used to run."

"Right, Mom. If you say so."

The Mom grinned and waved her off, shuffling toward the kitchen. "Go get 'em, kid. I've got coffee to make."

Harper put in her earbuds and pushed play. It was always such a deal with The Mom. Either they were fighting over stupid little shit or they were trying to get along while their jokes bounced off each other like beach balls, flying away without ever making solid contact. Harper went downstairs and out through the front door, already running down the front walk by the time the door slammed shut behind her. It was still cool and dewy, but you could tell it was going to be hot later in the day. Harper found her stride and fell into the rhythm of the run. She felt her dream of Sofie Helle receding with each block she covered and decided on a long, ten-mile run. Yeah. She'd run out to Burbling Brook and pay a surprise visit to her grandmother. She'd run south, toward the mountains, and take a break from Hawthorn for a while.

She was the summer wind, sweeping across the land.

She was The Harper.

———

The streets of Hawthorn dropped away as Harper made her way through her favorite running playlist—lots of bubblegum pop, with some kick-ass rock to shake things up once in a while—and the Clawhook Mountains got a tiny bit bigger. Usually her phone chimed with a text or two from Eva, but it was still a few hours too early for her to be up. Harper wondered what her best friend had gotten up to after they'd left Kira Fredrickson's party. Eva was always talking shit about losing her virginity, but her parents were Catholic and her dad wouldn't let her go on the pill, which was crazy, and so far she'd (mostly) kept her pants on, though she was always talking about oral sex like it was her favorite hobby. Harper figured Eva was ninety percent bluster and ten percent action, but who knew, really? As soon as you thought you had Eva Alvarez pegged, she'd surprise you.

Harper approached the Hawthorn cemetery, which was

a mile outside of town and surrounded by an old iron fence and blue spruce trees planted along the fence line as a windbreak. An idea popped into her mind, and Harper turned off the highway and headed down the gravel access road to the cemetery's entrance. She went under the front gate, which had **HAWTHORN** imprinted on it in gold letters, and ran onto the cemetery grounds. She passed through the newer front section, still jogging, and didn't pull up until she got to the back section, where the gravestones were old and the chiseled inscriptions worn down by time. Some of the inscriptions were so difficult to read she had to touch the engraved lines to confirm their meaning.

Edward John Birling
b. 1863
d. 1872

Josephine Beatrice Carver
1874–1876
A Brief Life, but O So Bright!

Grace Mary Hayes
Died One Month Old
In the Year of Our Lord
Eighteen and Sixty-Nine

Harper touched the dead infant's inscription. It was worn but still surprisingly visible, as if whoever had chiseled the lettering had wanted to make certain it lasted a long time. Jesus. It had been ridiculously dangerous to be a baby back in the old days, not to mention a woman giving birth. Surviving to adulthood had been mostly about luck and stubbornly vigorous genetics. Nobody had handed out asthma inhalers or flu vaccinations, that was for sure. If you wanted to live, you needed to be lucky or really earn it.

A squirrel hopped up on Birling's gravestone, stared at Harper a second, and leapt away into the forest, zipping between the cemetery's fence as if it weren't there at all. Harper watched the squirrel's fluffy gray tail disappear into the trees before she continued her search, going slow and steady, but she couldn't find Sofie's grave. She found Astrid and Torvald Helle, though, and a woman named Gerta Firebrick who might have been Sofie's sister.

Harper touched Astrid Helle's gravestone and scanned the cemetery again.

"Where are you, Sofie? Where did you go?"

Harper shivered, even though it was getting warmer and she'd worked up a good sweat. She sighed and started running again, flying between the gravestones on her long legs, once again The Harper.

Harper discovered her grandmother standing at her bedroom window, dressed only in her underwear and bra. She was standing so still it was as if she'd been turned into a department store mannequin—a rare saggy senior citizen model—and for a moment Harper had wondered if time itself had stopped.

"I can hear you breathing," Grandma Spurling said, turning around and breaking the surreal spell. "You've been running, haven't you?"

Harper stepped into the room. Her endorphins had kicked in, and she was feeling good. More awake.

"Yep. I ran here all the way from the house. What were you looking at?"

Grandma Spurling turned back to the window. The flesh on her shoulders was loose and hung in pinched folds against her bra strap. Harper looked around for actual clothes, but nothing had been laid out yet. Every time she came out to visit, Grandma Spurling seemed a little odder. The last time Harper had visited, her grandmother hadn't bothered to shut the bathroom door when she used the toilet, talking to Harper through the open doorway as if it was a normal way to interact with your grandkid.

"I saw something in the trees," Grandma Spurling said. "Some kind of animal."

Harper came up and stood beside her grandmother. She couldn't see anything but a freshly mowed lawn and the usual pine trees.

"Maybe it was a deer."

"No," Grandma Spurling said, "it was bigger than that."

They stared out the window. Harper wondered if seeing mysterious critters in the woods was a sign of dementia. She hoped not.

Grandma Spurling sighed and went over to her closet. She took a brown dress off a hanger and pulled it on over her head. It was as if she was putting on a gunny sack with arm holes cut into it. For such a cool lady, Grandma Spurling had a terrible sense of style.

"You must be thirsty after a run like that."

"I am, actually," Harper said.

"Why don't you come into the dining room with me? We'll get you some water and a bagel. A growing girl like you needs fuel."

"Okay."

Harper followed her grandmother down the hallway to the dining room. They passed old folks in wheelchairs and old folks still lying in bed and old folks slowly making their way along with the help of a walker. Some of them smiled and said hello, and some scowled and stared at Harper with eyes that burned like cinders. It really wasn't that different from high school, except the smells were different. Less B.O. and more poo smell, really.

The dining room was mostly empty, the round tables occupied in one or two spots, almost everybody eating alone. Grandma Spurling got a tray of hot food from the kitchen window and talked the cook into an extra toasted bagel with cream cheese and a glass of water for Harper. They sat down at an empty table at the back of the dining hall in a spot of sunshine.

"So, how was the party last night?"

"Fun," Harper said, taking a bite of her bagel. "Until the boy who drove me there got all dodgy."

"Boys do get dodgy," Grandma Spurling said, stirring her scrambled eggs with her fork. "And just wait until they get older."

Harper took a big drink of water. She decided to eat only half the bagel since she still had the five-mile run home ahead of her.

"So we went to a hot tub party in the mountains, and everything was going great. The view was beautiful, the night was beautiful, and everybody was in a fun, relaxed mood. This boy and I were talking one-on-one and I felt like we were, you know, really connecting, but when I asked him if he wanted to kiss me, he froze up. I mean really froze up, like his face became this stiff mask. Then he said it was time for him to drive me back to town and BAM—that was it. He took me home like he wanted to get rid of me as soon as possible."

Grandma Spurling chopped her scrambled eggs into smaller and smaller bits with the side of her fork. Harper took another bite of bagel, remembering Olav's rusty car as it roared away into the dark night.

"Well, it sounds like your fella doesn't know what he wants right now," Grandma Spurling said. "Maybe he's gay."

Harper glanced at her grandmother. She hadn't thought of that.

"At your age, nobody really knows what they want out of their life," Grandma Spurling said, giving up on her eggs and removing the wrapper from the blueberry muffin on her tray. "Figuring out what you want is a big part of being young. That's really your number one job right now. Even all your schoolwork is about giving you enough information about the world to help you figure out what you want out of life."

"So I guess Olav doesn't want me."

"Olav?" Grandma Spurling said, picking off a piece of the muffin. "That's an old name. He must be Scandinavian."

"Olav Helle. His family is related to Sofie Helle."

"Really? That's interesting."

Her grandmother chewed the piece of muffin, thinking. Two old men in wheelchairs rolled into the dining room at the same time and crashed into each other. An old woman waved to their table from the opposite corner of the room with a big, medicated grin on her face. The dining room was filling up. Everybody looked at each other as if surprised they were all still hanging around and drinking orange juice.

"Just look at this lot," Grandma Spurling said, shaking her head. "It's the last charge of the Dingbat Brigade."

17

THAT EVENING HARPER had to babysit The
Brothers so The Mom and The Dad could go on their
monthly adults-only dinner and movie date. As always, The
Dad gave them twenty-five dollars for pizza and told them
not to break anything or burn the house down. The Dad
warned them every time not to burn the house down as if it
was something Harper had let happen before.

Cameron didn't think he needed a babysitter at all. As
soon as The Mom and The Dad left on their date, he sulked
around the house like he was in prison.

"I'm too old to be babysat!" he shouted, standing in
front of the TV.

"Move," Sam said. "We're trying to watch."

"Make me."

Harper checked her phone, hoping for something new
from Eva or Olav. Or basically anybody above the age of
ten.

"Cameron, move."

Cameron slapped his hands against his hips and jumped
onto the couch between Sam and Harper, making the
couch rock. Harper wondered if The Mom kept any valium
in the upstairs bathroom and how exactly she could slip it
to her brother. Crumble it into his soda? Slip it into his garlic bread? He ate so fast he'd probably snarf it right down.

"Just settle down," Harper said. "The pizza will be here soon."

Cameron groaned, but he was already looking at the TV again. They were watching a nature show, and some kind of hawk was gliding through the air, circling above a grassy field. The camera cut to a prairie gopher standing pertly at the edge of its hole, nibbling at something it had grasped between its paws. The hawk dove abruptly, dropping like a feathery missile. Harper thought it looked pretty badass, a streaking blur of wind-ruffled feathers, beak, and talons.

The camera cut to the prairie dog, still nibbling. What the hell was he eating, anyway? A single kernel of corn?

"Oh, no," Sam whispered. "Run."

The prairie dog stopped its nibbling and perked up its ears. The other prairie dogs, in the prairie dog town that evidently surrounded the single prairie dog's hole, were squeaking like crazy and ducking back into their holes. The nibbling prairie dog looked up like "Oh shit!" and dropped back into its hole right as the hawk came swooping in, talons extended. Having missed its target, the hawk swooped back into the sky and let out a piercing screech that must have caused every small animal in a ten-mile radius to crap its pants.

Cameron laughed and slapped his knee.

"Ha. Stupid hawk!"

Harper sighed and checked her phone again. She'd been cheering for the hawk.

The pizza delivery dude showed up from Panda Pies, but it wasn't Olav, just some greasy older dude Harper didn't know. They ate their pizza and garlic bread in front of the TV and watched *Jaws*, which none of them had ever seen before. Sam and Cameron cheered for the shark and shouted encouragement to it whenever it swam on-screen. By the time the movie ended, The Brothers were so spazzed up Harper made them go outside and play in the backyard while she sat on the patio and read articles on her phone.

The sky grew darker as the sun set, turning a deeper blue. Harper didn't notice the figure standing in the backyard, near the corner of their house, until he coughed into his hand.

"Jesus," Harper said, jerking upright in her chair. Olav Helle waved and took a few steps toward the patio.

"Sorry," he said. "I tried the front door, but nobody answered. I heard shouting back here, so I thought I'd check it out."

Cameron and Sam were messing around in the spruce trees that ran along the far edge of their backyard, shooting each other with water rifles and arguing about who was dead and who was alive. They were oblivious to the visitor and anything else not related to their game. They could go for hours like that.

Harper set her phone down on the table and leaned back in her chair. Olav rubbed the side of his head.

"I'm sorry about last night, Harper. Sometimes I get freaked out for no reason."

"You do?"

"Yeah. It happens a lot at school. Sometimes right in the middle of class."

Olav looked at the tree line. Harper couldn't see The Brothers, but she could still hear them shouting. Now the sky was going from deep blue to purplish black, and it wasn't so hot anymore. It was the kind of perfect summer night you thought about in the middle of January, when the wind came howling down from the Clawhooks and rattled your bedroom windows.

Olav came up to the edge of the brick patio. "I'll be sitting there trying to pay attention, right? Listening to the teacher talking? And suddenly my heart starts beating faster and my throat swells up and I look around the classroom and I'm like, *who the hell are these people*? Why am I sitting with these strangers listening to some bullshit about Vietnam or *To Kill a Mockingbird*?"

Harper nodded, though she didn't exactly get what he was talking about. She liked history. She liked *To Kill a Mockingbird*.

"I don't know," Olav said. "I guess my brain's fucked up."

Harper cupped her elbows and felt her anger fade. So he hadn't wanted to kiss her in the hot tub. So what? It was his life.

"That's okay," Harper said. "My brain is kind of fucked up, too."

"It is?"

"Yeah. I'm basically obsessed with your ancestor."

"You mean Sofie?"

"I went to the cemetery today and tried to find her

grave. I walked basically every single row, but she's not even buried out there."

Olav frowned.

"Huh. Weird."

Sam yelped in the distance, and Olav frowned in a serious, thoughtful way. Harper uncrossed her arms. "Have a seat," she said, nodding at the chair beside her. Olav, looking properly relieved, sat down beside her at the patio table. They watched the trees together. Cameron's head flashed through the branches and disappeared again as he gave a war screech, crashing through the undergrowth like a wild boar.

"Are those your brothers?"

"Unfortunately," Harper said, pretending to look casually at her phone. "I'm babysitting them while my parents are on a date."

"That's cool. I always wished I had brothers. I'm an only child."

Harper laughed and coughed into her hand. "Oh, man. That's a good one."

Olav glanced sidelong at her, puzzled.

"Trust me. My little brothers are insane. They drive me crazy every freaking day."

Sam popped out of the trees and stared at them.

"Who's that?"

"My friend," Harper said. "Olav."

"Is he your boyfriend?"

Harper glanced at Olav.

"You see what I mean? They're insane."

Sam disappeared into the trees again without waiting for an answer. A fresh round of battle shouts rang out, sending a bunch of startled birds soaring into the air. It was getting dark faster now. She'd have to call The Brothers inside soon.

Harper turned toward Olav, who was watching her with those bright blue eyes of his. Those eyes weren't even fair.

"What?" she asked.

"I think you're really pretty, Harper," Olav said, speaking casually, like he'd just told her what time it was.

"Oh yeah?"

Olav nodded and leaned toward her. "I know I messed up when you asked me last night, but can I kiss you now?"

"Um, okay."

"Are you sure?"

"Yeah."

Olav leaned in closer and kissed her. Harper felt a shivery POP on her lips, and then she was kissing him back. It was nice at first, but then she realized Olav kissed like he was snarling, as if he didn't know whether he actually wanted to kiss her or bite her.

Harper pulled back. Her lips buzzed as if they'd just touched a live electrical wire.

"Have you ever had a girlfriend before?"

"No," Olav said. "That was my first kiss."

Harper smoothed her hair and looked across the backyard. The Brothers had gone silent. She wouldn't be surprised if they were watching right now, giggling as they spied, trying not to make too much noise. "We can see you guys," Harper called out, bluffing in case her brothers actually were watching. Something fluttered out of the trees and flew across the lawn toward the patio. Harper thought it might be a bat at first, but as it got closer she realized it was a moth—a pure white moth the size of her own hand. It rose and fell as its white wings beat against the soft night air. It landed on the table in front of Olav.

"Wow," Harper said, smiling as she leaned forward to get a closer look. "That's so pretty. It's like a ghost moth."

Harper flinched as Olav's hand shot forward and caught the moth by one wing, pinching it between his fingers. He moved so fast Harper didn't have time to say anything before he grabbed its other wing and pulled the moth apart, ripping off its wings and letting its body drop onto the patio table, where it writhed frantically.

Harper pushed her chair back and shot to her feet. "Fuck, dude! What the fuck is wrong with you!?"

Olav looked at her, both wings still fluttering in his hands.

"What? It's just a bug."

Harper stared at him. His eyes were flat and emotionless. He wasn't kidding. He wasn't trying to mess with her or show off in some kind of dude way. He really didn't get it.

"I think you should go," Harper said, so angry the patio seemed to spin around her, all her warm feelings suddenly turning sour.

"Okay."

Olav got up and released the moth's wings, which caught the breeze and fluttered away. He walked across the lawn without looking back and disappeared around the corner of the house. The wingless moth kept writhing on the table. Harper's mind whirled, still trying to figure out what the hell had just gone down. She shouted for her brothers to come inside and crossed her arms, shivering despite the warm summer air.

The last of the daylight faded as Sam and Cameron emerged from the trees and walked toward the house. Harper flicked the moth's body off the table and stepped on it with her flip-flop, smooshing it out of its misery.

18

OLAV WALKED AROUND the house and down the Spurlings' driveway to his car, which he'd parked on the street. So. Harper Spurling liked moths, apparently, and she'd kicked him out of her yard.

And the way she'd looked at him was so . . .

Bitchy.

So fucking bitchy.

Olav got into his car and started its engine. He pulled away from the Spurlings' house and continued down the street, rolling down his window and lighting a cigarette. It was a beautiful night, he thought. Why not go for a drive?

Why not visit the mountains?

Olav ditched his car a half mile down the road from Kira Fredrickson's cabin and continued the rest of the way on foot, letting his crowbar dangle loosely from his fingers. The mountain air was colder than in town, and he could smell the snow that never completely melted off the peak of Mount Pale. He was wearing only a T-shirt and jeans, and the night chill caused goosebumps to rise on his bare forearms. He didn't mind. The cold balanced the killing heat in his mind, and he was able to think clearly, as clearly as he ever had before a kill. This would be the first time he'd picked his victim out ahead of time instead of allowing the moment to simply happen. This would be the first time he killed somebody he knew personally. This would be Number Six.

The lights were on in Kira's cabin. Olav walked up her driveway, using the starlight to guide him, and listened carefully for the sound of voices. He expected to encounter another keg party, since she'd said her parents were out of town for three or four more days, but the night was silent except for the whooo-ing of a single owl. Olav circled around the front of the cabin, careful to stay in the shadows, and went around to the backyard, where the hot tub and the bonfire pit were set up. Lawn chairs were spread out in the yard and beer cans littered the grass, but nobody was outside. Olav circled around the house's other side and peered through each window until he came to the living room, where he could clearly see Kira and her boyfriend lying on a couch and watching TV.

What was her boyfriend's name again?

Josh something?

Olav placed the crowbar behind him and arced his back, stretching out a few vertebrae. They were watching TV, and they were *his* TV at the same time. The coffee table had a bong on it and a bunch of empty beer bottles, and the TV's light flickered on their slack, stoned-looking faces. Olav wondered if they'd start to have sex sooner or later or if he'd already missed that part of the show. He wondered what it would be like, sitting with your girlfriend on a couch in a cozy mountain cabin, high and happy and thinking you were the only two people around for miles. He pressed the crowbar across his crotch and began to stroke it, enjoying the feel of the hardened steel against the palm of his hand.

———————

Time passed.

Olav wanted to check his phone, but he didn't dare risk the light giving him away.

This was hunting.

You didn't fuck around when you were hunting.

———————

Josh closed his eyes and lay down on the couch, putting his feet in his girlfriend's lap. Kira massaged them absentmindedly, absorbed in whatever was on TV. The intensity of the flickering light increased on her face and then stopped entirely. Kira shook her head as if waking from a dream and said something to Josh, who didn't move. She raised his feet off her lap and stood up, dropping his feet back onto the couch. Josh still didn't move. Kira said something else, waited, and walked out of the part of the living room Olav could see. Olav headed around the house in the same direction, caught a brief view of her in another window, still moving, and followed her to the back of the house.

Nothing happened for a minute, and Olav wondered if he'd guessed wrong and Kira had gone to bed or something. He was still holding the crowbar, and its weight was making his right shoulder ache faintly, the kind of ache you got when you fired a rifle a few times. This was better, he realized. Hunting like this was better than the random kills. The easy kills.

The cabin's back door opened and Kira stepped outside, carrying a wine cooler and a towel. Olav stayed back in the shadows and watched as she walked over to the hot tub, pulled off the bulky foam lid, and laid it against the side of the tub. She set her wine cooler and towel on the edge of the tub and activated the tub's jets, which started churning the water immediately and created a welcome blanket of white noise. Kira took off her shirt and sweatpants, revealing a two-piece swimsuit beneath, and swung a leg over the edge of the tub.

Kira looked in Olav's direction for a moment, and he was worried he'd been spotted standing there in the dark. But no, she was thinking, waiting for her leg to get used to the hot water. She swung her other leg over the edge of the tub and slipped inside it, grimacing as she lowered herself fully into the water.

Olav waited for Kira to get settled in before he circled around and approached the hot tub from behind. He could see only her sandy blond head, bobbing above the edge of the tub. She reached out, grabbed the wine cooler from the ledge, and twisted off its cap. Olav raised the crowbar above his head but waited, letting her have the drink, letting her enjoy one more sweet thing. He looked up at the clear night sky. This would do it, he realized. This would finally appease the stars, and they would tell the skull where the Doorway was—their mission would soon be complete.

Olav gathered himself and brought the crowbar down with all his strength. He felt the steel bar parting the air, the very molecules of the summer night, and then connect solidly with the crown of Kira Fredrickson's skull.

CRACK.

She slumped forward immediately into the hot tub's churning water. Olav waited for her to start thrashing, to fight for her life, but a minute passed and all she did was float there, face down in the water, which was turning pink with blood. He reached into the tub and fished Kira's body out. He slumped her onto the tub's seat and checked her pulse with two fingers, as he'd done to so many deer lying broken and twisted on the side of the road.

She was gone.

Number Six was in the bag.

"Thank you," Olav said, leaning forward and kissing the dead girl on the lips. He closed his eyes and imagined he was kissing Harper Spurling.

It wasn't hard to do.

Part Three

19

THE KEEGANS LIVED three blocks away. Harper and her mother walked the short distance to their house despite the afternoon heat, their arms laden with a plastic bowl of fruit salad, a loaf of bread wrapped in tinfoil, and an aluminum tray of lasagna. It was a lazy Saturday in Hawthorn, and July was only a few days away. The air smelled like pine sap warmed by sunlight, grilled meat, and freshly cut grass.

Kira Fredrickson had been dead for a week, and Harper still had a hard time believing her friend was dead. She'd attended both the wake and the funeral. She'd seen Kira laid out in her favorite purple dress, her face covered in makeup and her hands crossed over her chest, and she *still* had a hard time believing Kira was dead. Harper had sat in the fifth row during the funeral, along with Eva and a bunch of other kids in their grade. The whole time she'd expected Kira to sit up, shout April fools, and hop out of the coffin with a big fooled-you grin on her face.

But no.

Her skull really had been fractured.

She'd really been found in a hot tub filled with her own blood, only one day after Harper had borrowed her swimsuit, and Josh Keegan was sitting in jail, under arrest for her murder.

"I hope they like lasagna," The Mom said, shifting the tray in her arms. "This wasn't maybe the best choice for summertime."

"Don't worry," Harper said. "Everybody loves lasagna."

"Do they?"

"Oh yeah. It's the perfect cheese delivery system."

The Mom pursed her lips and frowned. They'd come up the Keegans' front walk and stopped at their doorstep. The Keegans' house was a white two-story Victorian that didn't look much different than their own house.

"What if they have gluten allergies?"

"I guess we'll just have to take that chance."

Harper, who was carrying only the fruit salad and the bread, stepped up and rang the Keegans' doorbell. She saw a flash of movement through the door's little side window and stepped back.

"Somebody's home."

The Mom grimaced and blew a puff of air into her bangs. She was sweaty from the walk, but Harper thought it made her look good. Like she'd just gotten back from the gym and was glowing with health.

A bolt turned, and the Keegans' front door opened. Mrs. Keegan peered out at them, looking dazed.

"Can I help you?"

The Mom stepped forward.

"It's me, Nancy. Beth Spurling."

Mrs. Keegan blinked, looking from The Mom to Harper. She had dark rings beneath her eyes. She was dressed in yoga pants and an old sweatshirt with grease stains on it.

"Oh. Hello."

Harper lifted up the fruit salad and bread she was carrying. "We brought food."

Mrs. Keegan looked at Harper as if she'd just spoken in tongues.

"Oh. Thank you . . ."

"Harper. I'm in Josh's grade."

"Right. I thought you looked familiar. You're on the track team with him."

"Yep. He's our best hurdler."

The Mom shifted on her feet. Mrs. Keegan stared at them for another long moment, as if her brain had just reset. She smiled and stepped back.

"Please. My husband isn't home right now, but you're welcome to come in."

The Mom and Harper exchanged a look. The Mom went inside first, cradling the tray of lasagna. The Keegans' house was dim, with the curtains drawn and none of the lights turned on. Mrs. Keegan led them to a living room littered with plush throw blankets, balled up tissue paper, and empty wine bottles. Mrs. Keegan sat down on the couch and covered her lap with a blanket. The Mom headed for the kitchen. "I'll just put the food in the fridge," she said, smiling brightly as she looked back over her shoulder. "This should really be refrigerated."

Mrs. Keegan nodded but didn't say anything. She was acting like a zombie.

"It's the medication," Mrs. Keegan said, as if she could read Harper's mind. "I'm on a lot of medication right now."

Harper smiled uneasily and followed her mother into the kitchen. The sink and countertops were piled with dirty dishes, and the garbage was overflowing. The refrigerator, however, was almost empty. The tray of lasagna fit easily on the middle shelf, and Harper set the garlic bread and the bowl of fruit salad on the top shelf beside a bottle of cranberry juice. The bread didn't need to be refrigerated, but it'd probably get lost and forgotten if she put it on the counter with all the dirty dishes.

"I don't think this was such a good idea," Harper whispered, shutting the refrigerator door. "They don't look like they want visitors."

The Mom gave her a look and started lifting the sides of the garbage bag up and tying it closed. She lifted the stuffed bag out of the bin and leaned it against the wall. She opened the cabinet doors beneath the sink, dug around for a second, and pulled out a fresh trash bag.

"They don't know what they want, Harper," The Mom whispered back. "Look around. They're in shock."

"But we hardly even know them."

"Nancy's purchased two of my paintings. Her son is on your track team."

"Her murderer son," Harper said, raising her voice.

The Mom glared at her. "That hasn't been proven, Harper, and you know that," she said, still whispering. "Josh is innocent until proven guilty. Besides, even if he did kill

Kira, his parents aren't responsible. Though I'm sure everybody in town is treating them like they have the plague."

"I know—"

"Then hush."

The Mom lined the trash bin with the new bag and handed the stuffed one to Harper.

"Take this out to the garage."

Harper sighed and took the bag. She carried the bloated thing with both hands, passing through the living room again on her way to the house's side door. She opened the garage door and flicked on the light. Josh's old beater of a truck was parked beside a newer-looking Toyota Corolla. Harper dropped the garbage into the big plastic bin and went back inside the house. The Mom was clearing off the coffee table in the living room and carrying everything back into the kitchen. Mrs. Keegan was still sitting in the same place on the couch, staring straight ahead with a blanket on her lap.

Harper sat beside her and took Mrs. Keegan's hand. They sat in silence and listened to glasses and dishware clink as The Mom did her thing in the kitchen. Mrs. Keegan's hand felt small and dry in Harper's grasp, like an acorn that could easily be crushed.

"I'm sorry about your friend Kira," Mrs. Keegan said, her voice soft but clearer now. "What happened to her was a horrible thing."

Harper felt a lump in her throat. She and Kira hadn't even been the greatest friends, but still. It was a horrible way to die.

"Thank you."

Mrs. Keegan turned on the couch and looked Harper straight in the eye. "He didn't do it," she said, her voice firm and certain. "Josh didn't murder Kira."

"He didn't?"

"No," Mrs. Keegan said, shaking her head. "He loved her more than anything."

———————

That night Harper went to bed early, exhausted by their mercy visit to the Keegans and the energy it had required just to sit with Mrs. Keegan. In fact, the whole week since she'd gone to Kira's cabin in the mountains had been exhausting, and she hadn't even seen Olav Helle around town, though she still thought about him every now and then and wondered if she'd overreacted to him killing the moth. She'd always known boys liked to kill bugs—just look at the stuff Cameron and Sam did—but the casual way Olav had plucked the moth apart still troubled her. Olav was sixteen. He should have grown out of that crap by now. He should have known you left the pretty, harmless bugs alone.

Harper fell asleep almost right away but woke up in the middle of the night, her mind clear and totally alert, as if she'd been awake for hours. She sat up in her bed, wondering if her cell phone had buzzed. She noticed her bedroom was unusually cold again, as if she was sleeping inside an industrial freezer, and she felt a chill in her toes.

Harper's breath caught in her throat. A figure was sitting at the foot of her bed. It was hard to make out any details in the pitch dark, but Harper could definitely tell something was there, darker than the darkness around it.

"Hello?"

The figure turned its head slightly, watching her.

Harper.

Harper shivered. She couldn't tell if she'd heard her name spoken aloud or if it was only in her head. Or if she'd heard it some way that was different than either. She pulled the covers up to her chin, as if a layer of blankets could protect her now.

Find me, the figure said.

Find me.

Harper swallowed.

"Sofie?"

The figure stood up and drifted backward, merging into the regular dark. Harper cautiously reached out and turned on the lamp beside her bed. Light flooded the room, which was empty except for her usual bedroom stuff.

Harper threw back the covers and stood up.

Her bedroom was still freezing.

20

SOMEHOW HARPER FELL back asleep around dawn. When she got up for good, it was already ten a.m. and her family had left for church. Harper, who had a serious story to tell, decided to visit her grandmother at Burbling Brook. By the time she got there, the assisted-living center's outdoor promenade was packed with old folks and their visiting relatives. Sunday morning was the facility's liveliest time of the week. The south porch, with its coveted view of the Clawhook Mountains, was so crowded that Harper and her grandmother were forced to sit on the west porch and look out at the Hawthorn cemetery in the distance.

"Sorry I didn't get here earlier," Harper said. "I know you like the south porch."

Grandma Spurling, who'd grown a little thinner over the past few weeks, was cocooned in a thick porch blanket despite the summer heat. "I don't mind this porch," she said. "I like to sit out here and watch the big storms coming in from the west. They try to make me come inside, but I stay until I feel the rain on my skin."

Harper nodded. "I bet the storms are really beautiful. All that open space."

Grandma Spurling smiled weakly. Harper could tell she was still groggy from her morning meds. The light in her eyes, that mental focus light, kept going in and out as if a short circuit was occurring somewhere in the web of her mental wiring.

The focus light came back.

"Well, Harper, what's the rest of the family doing today?"

"They're at church getting their weekly dose of Jesus," Harper said. "Mom said she'll stop by later with a pie."

"That's right, it's Sunday, isn't it? I keep forgetting what day it is."

An old woman with her hair in curlers slowly shuffled past them, making the rounds with her walker. "Lila Riley's such a goddamn show-off," Grandma Spurling grumbled. "She parades out here every day like she's running a marathon and we should all cheer."

"You could buy her a medal."

"Ha. And I could pin it on her fat ass."

Harper grinned, happy at this evidence that the old Grandma Spurling fire was still burning. Harper had once seen her grandma ream out a biker for letting a restaurant door slam instead of holding it open for her.

"Mom and I visited Josh Keegan's mother yesterday," Harper said. "She says he's innocent. She says Josh loved Kira."

Grandma Spurling turned to look at Harper.

"Do you know Josh well?"

Harper shrugged. "He's a dude. He's always seemed nice enough. I've never heard anything weird about him."

"I'm sure he's nice," Grandma Spurling said, nodding. "But we all know what nice can hide, don't we?"

Lila passed them again with her walker, smiling like she'd won a million dollars. Harper's grandmother didn't say anything for a few minutes, and Harper studied her from the corner of her eye.

"Can I tell you something, Grandma?"

"Of course, dear."

"It's pretty weird."

Grandma Spurling smiled. "I like weird, Harper."

"All right." Harper tucked a loose strand of hair behind her ear. "You know how I've been reading that diary of a pioneer girl? *The Diary of Sofie Helle*? Well, last night I woke up in the middle of the night and it was freezing in my room. Really freezing. I sat up and saw someone at the foot of my bed."

Harper swallowed, remembering the shadowy figure. How it somehow seemed there and not there at the same time. How it stood out from the darkness. Darker than dark.

"It was Sofie Helle, Grandma. I couldn't see her face, but I just *knew* it was her."

Grandma Spurling looked up at the sky. It was cloudy, though it didn't look like it was going to rain. Harper laced her fingers together and flexed her forearms.

"I said hello, but Sofie didn't say anything right away. She just turned to look at me, called my name, and then said, 'Find me' two times and melted back into the dark.

When I turned on my lamp, she was gone, but my room was still freezing cold."

Grandma Spurling blinked her eyes.

"Well. That's some story, dear."

"I know, right? I don't know if I'm going crazy or maybe I was just dreaming within a dream or something."

Harper scrutinized her grandmother. The deep lines in her face. Her pale eyes.

"Do you believe in ghosts, Grandma?"

Harper's grandmother slipped a hand out from beneath her blanket wrap and gestured down the porch, where smiley-faced Lila was still plugging along with her walker while the other residents did their best to ignore her.

"When you get old enough, Harper, you start to feel how thin the veil is. I've had mornings recently where I woke up unsure if I was still alive. When I look in the mirror, I can almost see through my own body. So, yes, I wouldn't be surprised if our souls slip back to this side of things on occasion. I wouldn't be surprised at all."

Harper nodded.

"Cool. I knew you'd believe me."

Grandma Spurling reached out and squeezed Harper's knee. "The question is, how are you going to find Sofie?"

"Well, I've tried," Harper said. "I've been to every Hawthorn history site there is. There's almost nothing about her except what's in the diary. She doesn't even have a gravestone in the cemetery. Her family's buried there but not her."

"Interesting. What about the library?"

"Huh?"

"The Hawthorn library. Were you able to find anything about her there?"

Harper sat up.

"Shit. I forgot about the library."

Grandma Spurling clucked her tongue and grinned, some of that old grandma sparkle back in her eyes. Behind her, Harper could see Lila Riley coming around the corner of the building, hell-bent on one more trip around the porch.

Actually, Harper decided, she was kind of starting to like Lila Riley.

21

AFTER A WEEK of silence, Olav knew the skull's presence was back as soon as it returned to his bedroom, though the skull itself still sat on his closet shelf and didn't look any different. Olav felt the skull's return as surely as he would have felt his mother or father entering the room, even if he had a blindfold on and they'd come in on tiptoe. The skull had been silent since the night of Kira Fredrickson's hot tub party, but now, yes, it was back.

Your sixth kill was your finest, the skull said.

Not *Hello, Olav* or *I'm back.*

Nope.

Just *Your sixth kill was your finest.*

Olav turned onto his stomach and buried his head beneath his pillow. He wanted to go back to sleep. He'd gotten used to the skull's absence. He'd gotten used to being alone again and untroubled.

The stars have finally been appeased. They have revealed the Doorway's location.

Nobody had discovered the fishing boy's body yet, and Olav hadn't killed anyone since Kira Fredrickson. He hadn't felt the killing urge. He'd been busy delivering pizzas and trying to decide if he wanted to go to college in another year. He'd come to think maybe killing six people was enough. Like it was a phase he'd gone through and now he could return to regular living. Besides, Josh Keegan was taking the blame for Kira, and maybe if they sent him to jail that would be enough to throw the cops off Olav's scent for good. Maybe he could figure out a way for Josh to get blamed for all the murders. Josh could be the Tender Heart Killer.

Olav rolled over and looked at the skull.

Go away, Olav thought. *I don't want to help you anymore.*

The choice is not yours.

Olav reburied his head beneath his pillow. He yawned, trying to will himself back to sleep. A grinding sound started in the back of his head, like something was digging through the back of his skull. His stomach started to hurt.

You must help me.

"No."

The grinding got louder. His stomach hurt more.

You must.

Olav curled in on himself and gritted his teeth. Nausea rippled through him. The bed felt as if it was heaving beneath him. He was in a tiny boat on a big, stormy ocean.

You MUST.

Olav opened his mouth and puked into his pillow. He flung the pillow across the room, coughing the puke chunks out. The grinding had turned into a high-pitched drilling, and little white dots fizzled and popped in his vision.

You MUST you MUST you MUST—

"Fine," Olav shouted, swinging his legs over the side of the bed. "Just shut up."

The drilling noise stopped, and his stomach unclenched. Olav thought he might puke a second time.

Yes, the skull said. *You must dig me up.*

"What?"

All of me.

You must reclaim all of me.

Olav groaned and stood up, looking for his jeans. He was regretting running over the neighbor's stupid cat more and more every day.

Olav fetched a shovel from the garage and crossed his backyard, carrying the skull in a large duffle bag. He entered the tree line at the edge of his yard and headed for the Clearing. He wondered what it would be like to be dead.

Death is like a dream in which you manage to pass through the world without a body. You are reduced to your will and your memories. There is no wind. There is no fire or snow or the smell of damp soil after it rains.

Olav entered the Clearing and set the duffle bag on the ground. He unzipped the bag and set the skull on the boulder in the middle of the Clearing. He circled around the rock, trying to remember exactly where he'd buried the cat. The ground around the boulder was covered in a bed of pine needles and appeared more or less even. He tapped around with the shovel until he found a loose spot in the soil. He plunged the shovel into the ground and started digging. The forest grew hushed and inert around him, as if all the birds and critters had been lulled into sleep.

He dug up Cooper first. The cat looked deader than ever, its skeleton covered in ants and a few rotting scraps of dirty fur. Olav tossed the dead cat out of the hole and kept digging until he struck something hard. He scraped more dirt away and a long yellow bone appeared. A femur. He dug around the bone and discovered it was a full skeletal leg with a foot.

I was quartered while still alive, the skull said, looking down on him from the Clearing's boulder. *That leg was cleaved first.*

"Why did they quarter you?"

We were at war.

"With who?"

Ourselves.

"Why?"

Because there was no one else to war with.

Olav lifted the leg out of the hole and set it to the side. He kept digging and soon found a second leg, followed by a ribcage still connected to a spine and hip bones. Then came two arms with the bony hands still attached, their fingers much longer than normal fingers and sharpened into points. Then he uncovered a bunch of pointy teeth, scattered about like seeds. Then the skull's missing jawbone, with a few pointy teeth still in their sockets.

Olav retrieved all these bones from the hole and set them to the side.

I cannot rest until I have returned through the Doorway.

Even if you crushed my remains to dust, I would still find no peace. I must rejoin the others.

Olav dug some more and sifted through the dirt. He found several more chunks of bone and added them to the pile.

That is all, the skull said. *You have found every piece.*

"Good," Olav said, tossing the shovel out of the hole and climbing out himself. He rolled onto his back and looked up at the sky. The light had changed. He'd been digging for hours, he realized. Through the morning and into the afternoon. He was hungry and thirsty, and his back ached. He pulled out his phone and checked the time. It was 1:30 already. It was as if he'd been possessed.

Your labor is almost done.

Olav got to his feet and brushed the dirt off his clothes as best he could. He stuffed the pile of bones into the duffle bag, starting with the ribcage/spine/hipbone piece first because it was the largest. It was as though he'd dug up a puzzle from the earth.

There is one more piece you will need to bring to the Doorway.

"A piece of you, you mean?"

No. You will need a sacrifice. Otherwise they will take you. They will be hungry.

Olav looked at the skull and then up at the sky.

"A person to sacrifice, you mean."

Yes. Someone you can draw to the valley without suspicion. The sacrifice must be alive until they are absorbed.

Olav picked up the skull and set it inside the duffle bag with the rest of the bones. He zipped the bag shut and grabbed the shovel. He footed Cooper back over the edge of the hole. He remembered the white moth he'd pulled apart in Harper Spurling's backyard and the look of horror and disgust she'd given him, like he was some kind of ugly alien. Like she regretted ever kissing him in the first place.

"Okay," Olav said. "I think I know somebody."

The Dead Man's Horse
(1866)

By the summer of 1866, Sofie Helle had turned sixteen and was now as tall as her mother. She'd received a silver necklace for her birthday, ordered from a catalogue and shipped all the way from out East. The necklace's charm was a snow owl with her name engraved beneath its talons. She'd taken to spending her days alone in the woods with a notebook so she could sketch wildlife as she came across it. She enjoyed all the animals and birds but found herself especially captivated by insects. Ants, termites, darkling beetles—they went at their labors with their entire beings, feeling neither joy nor sadness.

Sofie often thought of the outlaw Crack Donegan, whom she'd buried in the forest three years before. She wondered what he'd feared so much as to take his life and frequently visited his burial spot in the forest. Sitting cross-legged beside his grave, Sofie would report to Mr. Donegan about the current events in town—such as the Dennison Mining Company, which had arrived in the area recently and was now blasting away for copper only a few miles distant in the Clawhook Mountains—and the wider world. Mr. Donegan never replied, being dead and in the ground, but he was a good listener, and Sofie found their one-sided conversations relaxing.

One day in late July, Sofie headed east into the forest and descended into the valley, thinking she'd spend the day in peaceful solitude, sketching the trees and the insects and perhaps find a sleeping owl or two. Instead she met with Everest Hahn, who was running through the forest at full tilt with his rifle in his hands. Everest—who was also sixteen—pulled up when he saw Sofie and stared at her for a long moment.

"Everest," Sofie said, eyeing the rifle. "What are you at out here?"

Everest swallowed. He was always tongue-tied around womenfolk, which amused the girls in town to no end. Broad-shouldered and thick in the cheeks, he was a handsome fellow in a burly German way.

"Hunting," Everest said, spitting the word out. "Don't tell your pa. I begged off sick from the timber crew."

"Hunting what?"

Everest shrugged.

"Everything."

"So is that why you were crashing through the forest like a wild boar?"

Everest shook his head.

"No. I was running back to town."

"Why is that?"

"I found a horse," Everest said, glancing over his shoulder. "And a cave."

"Oh? A horse got loose from town?"

"No," Everest said, looking back over his shoulder. "I don't think it's one of ours. It was mighty strange. It was standing outside a cave all stiff like. The horse looked starved, but it wouldn't come to me. Like it had turned savage."

"Savage?" Sofie's heart thudded loudly in her chest. It couldn't be the same horse. Not after three years.

"Show me where this horse is," she whispered, grabbing Everest Hahn by the shoulders. "Show me now."

"But—"

"Everest Hahn," Sofie said, using her mother's stern tone, "you show me this horse and this cave if you want to live to dinner."

Everest nodded his head and swallowed.

"Yes, ma'am."

They went down the hillside and into the densely wooded valley. Sofie felt hot, like her blood had been warmed on the stove. She would try to capture the horse and take it home. She would feed it and groom it and nurture it back to health.

They crossed the valley and neared the ridge on the other side. Everest, who spent his every free minute hunting in the valley, used the ridgeline as his marker as he retraced his steps. Sofie saw the cave before Everest could point it out and ran ahead. The cave's entrance was small and fitted nearly perfectly into the hillside—if she hadn't been looking for it she would have walked right past it.

"Sofie, wait!"

Sofie pulled up at the edge of the tree line, close enough to the cave that she could have tossed a rock into it. Everest ran up behind her, bumping into her hard enough that she almost fell over, but Sofie hardly noticed the collision. A horse was standing outside the cave's entrance.

Crack Donegan's horse.

The runaway.

"It's you," Sophie whispered. "You're still alive."

The horse was scrawnier than she remembered, nearly a skeleton on four legs. Its dark eyes looked enormous against the drawn flesh of its face, and a cloud of black flies swarmed around its hindquarters. It looked terrible and ugly. Like it shouldn't even have been alive.

The horse raised its head and sniffed the air. It could smell her.

Sofie emerged from the trees.

"Hey there, horsey. Remember me?"

The horse swung its head toward her and snorted. It was a rough, unfriendly sound. A menacing sound. The horse pawed the ground and lowered its bony head in their direction, as if it was considering charging. Sofie's throat tightened and she looked at Everest, who'd turned as pale as fresh snow.

"We should leave," Everest said, pulling on Sofie's arm. "It doesn't want us here."

The horse's tail swished at the cloud of flies buzzing around its hindquarters. This only agitated the flies into further swarming—their buzzing was so loud Sofie could hear it from where she was standing.

Sofie held out the palm of her hand and made a soft clucking sound. The horse snorted again and stepped sideways, revealing a large open wound on its side.

"Oh," Sofie whispered, cupping her mouth.

The wound was enormous and ragged, as if the horse had been swiped at by a bear, or set upon by wolves. So many flies had set upon it they appeared, from a distance, to form a black, scabrous bandage over it. A living dressing.

"What did that, Everest?"

"I don't know," Everest said. "But whatever it was, it's still out here somewhere, I reckon."

Sofie took another step forward. A cold wind gusted out from inside the cave, carrying the sick smell of the horse with it. Why was the horse hovering here? There was no grass to feed on. No pool of water to drink from.

"Horsey, horsey," Sofie called out, stepping within a few yards of the spindly creature. "Let us take you home and help you."

Crack Donegan's horse swung round and rose up on its hind legs, whinnying loudly as it pawed the air, its hooves passing so close to Sofie's face she could feel the air disturbed against her cheek. She fell backward onto the ground, her entire body stiff with fear.

The horse's front legs thudded back to the earth, throwing a cloud of dust in their direction.

It didn't want help.

It didn't want them near the cave.

"Enough," Everest said, lifting Sofie back to her feet and pulling her back toward the trees. Sofie turned her back on the mangled horse and followed the boy into the forest. She didn't know what terrors the horse had known in the woods, but it was no longer the same creature she'd encountered three years before.

———————

They returned to town. Sofie said goodbye to Everest and went her own way, intending to find her sister and tell her about the horse. Instead she discovered her father sitting beneath the town bridge, smoking his pipe and staring into the river.

"Papa?"

Torvald Helle raised his eyes from the river and considered his daughter. He did not seem surprised to see her. He looked tired, his eyes red and cracked. He was not such a spring chicken anymore, Sofie realized. He was on the edge of old age.

"Hello, daughter."

Sofie sat down beside her father, spreading her dress out beneath her on the grassy bank. The familiar burnt cherry smell of his pipe filled the air in a comforting way.

"What are you doing here, Papa? Why aren't you out working?"

Her father shrugged.

"I did not feel like it today."

"Are you sick?"

"No. Not particularly."

Sofie lowered her head and touched the owl charm hanging from her necklace. She recalled Crack Donegan's horse, pawing at the air with such fury.

Sofie reached out and took her father's hand. It was rough and deeply creased by all the years of felling trees and hauling them into town. She recalled watching him drive the wagon on the long trip across the plains from St. Louis ten years before, when she'd been so little. Back then, he'd seemed like a giant capable of leading them any distance, wolves or no wolves. Now he was just a tired-looking man with silver in his beard, sitting beside a river.

"I have been thinking lately," her father said. "Maybe we were wrong to come here. Maybe this place is truly not meant for habitation. When I think of Baby William snatched by that wolf . . ."

Her father's eyes lost their focus. Sofie didn't say anything. Nearly her entire life had been spent in Hawthorn. She could not imagine living anywhere else.

Her father smiled sadly and patted Sofie's hand.

"But I guess our roots are too deep now, eh?"

Sofie leaned against her father's shoulder and stared into the river. She pictured Crack Donegan's sickly horse, its wound covered in a swarm of flies. How could the world be so dreadful and so beautiful at the same time?

A silver fish leapt out of the river, flashing brilliantly in the sunlight before it disappeared from sight. "I should have brought my fishing pole," Sofie's father said, knocking the char from the bowl of his pipe. Sofie didn't say anything in reply, and they watched the river in companionable silence, lost in their own thoughts.

It was beautiful, watching all that dark water flow past.

22

THE HAWTHORN TOWN library was open only from noon to four on Sundays. Harper got there at eleven, banged uselessly on the entrance doors, and walked two blocks away to a coffee shop to kill some time. She couldn't believe she'd spaced on the whole library-as-a-resource angle. The Dad would have loved to hear about this. He was always going on about how people were neglecting books and frying their brains on the Internet and spending all their time staring down at glowing screens like zombies.

Harper ordered a vanilla mocha with a shot of caramel and took it over to a tiny window table. The shop was buzzing with customers, and she was lucky to find a spot (apparently everyone in Hawthorn who wasn't going to church or visiting Burbling Brook had decided to get as highly caffeinated as possible). She took her phone out and saw she'd gotten a text from Eva, who seemed highly caffeinated herself.

Hey Harp where you at?

Billy's Bean. I'm waiting for the library to open

We have a LIBRARY?

I know. Crazy, right?

Libraries are so hot

WTF?

Oh yeah. They're on my sex list

Not that stupid list again

Sex in the stacks! You'd have to be so quiet grrrrr

U r such a freak

Why @ library?

Research

Oh god is this about Sofie Helle?

Maybe

I knew it! Sexy dead girl research!

Whatever

So you want to meet for Chinese after? I want to eat a million
    spring rolls

K. How about 2?

K. C u later

Harper set her phone on the table and sipped her mocha, enjoying the frothy coffee taste and instant sugar high. She looked around the coffee shop and suddenly felt hyperaware of every single person in the room. The two ladies in workout clothes. The sweet old couple reading the paper across from each other. The dude with chunky glasses who was reading a huge book while sipping a cappuccino. The four ladies sitting together and knitting while they chatted and laughed. They were all so . . . alive.

But temporary, too.

Like they were all just passing through.

Harper turned away and looked out the window beside her table. Orange and yellow leaves swirled down the street, carried by the wind. She could smell woodsmoke seeping through the window, mingling with the shop's roasting coffee-bean smell, and the smell made her think of winter and the mountains. A car drove by and a little boy with huge brown eyes stared at her from the backseat, his puffy cheeks flushed pink. Harper sipped her mocha and checked her phone. Time always seemed to pass too fast or too slowly. Time was never just right.

———————

Harper was waiting outside the library when an old guy with a bushy gray beard and round tortoiseshell glasses unlocked the front doors and flipped the closed sign to open. She'd finished her mocha, and now all her wires were humming.

"Hi," Harper said, approaching the librarian as he sat down behind the library's information counter. The lobby had a shiny polished floor and three tables with self-checkout scanners and two return drops built into the information counter. In one corner stood a bronze statue of a grim-looking dude in a buckskin coat and an old-timey hat, posed with one hand on his hip and a rifle slung over his shoulder. At the base of the statue was a copper plate that read Eldon Hawthorn, one of the Five Founders.

"Good afternoon," the librarian said. "How can I help you?"

"Do you have any books on Sofie Helle?"

The librarian angled his head and peered at her through his thick glasses. He had tufts of white hair sticking out of his ears *and* his nose.

"You're doing a report for school?"

"Kind of. We actually read her diary in school last spring. I was wondering if you had anything, you know, more about her."

"Well, we have a few town histories written by local residents, but I don't think they mention her . . ."

"Oh."

"But we also have her original diary."

"No shit?!"

Harper covered her mouth.

"Whoops. Sorry."

"That's all right. It's only one of the old words." The librarian pushed his glasses up the bridge of his nose. "So, would you like to read the original diary?"

Harper nodded.

"Yes, please."

"Just a moment."

The librarian turned and left the counter, ducking into a back room that looked packed with metal carts and library materials. Harper moseyed across the lobby and studied the statue of Eldon Hawthorn more closely. He looked sad yet determined, like he'd seen a lot of bad shit but wasn't turning back, no matter what. Sofie had mentioned Eldon in her diary, how his baby was stolen by wolves and how his first wife had died in the woods and how he'd gotten remarried to a lady who wouldn't let him drink anymore. Real fun stuff, being a pioneer back in the day.

"Can you name the five founding families?"

The librarian had returned and was holding a leather-bound book that was sealed in a plastic bag.

"Well, I'm a Spurling, so there's one."

"Oh, really? Interesting."

"And I'm here about Sofie Helle, so that's two, and we can't forget about old Hawthorn over here, right?"

"Indeed."

Harper tapped her cheek, thinking. The two bars Sofie's dad was always drinking at. The Leather Boot and The Drunken Selkie.

"Hahn and Brodigan, right?"

The librarian grinned. "Very good! I don't know many folks who can name all five."

"Well, I'm kind of a big fan of Sofie's diary. I've read it about a dozen times."

"Oh? Then you should really enjoy reading the original item in her own handwriting." The librarian handed Harper the diary sealed in a plastic bag. "It's a special archives document, so you can only peruse it in the reading room. No food or drink while you read it, please."

Harper carried the diary through the stacks and went into the reading room. The reading room was a large, sunshine-filled space with a high ceiling lined with clerestory windows, like it was a reading church, and the walls beneath the windows were lined with map cabinets and shelves crammed with reference books. Harper picked a reading table at random and sat down. Nobody else was in the big room, and the silence was thick, like an invisible syrup you could feel if you swiped your hand through the air fast enough. Harper opened the plastic bag and took out the diary. It had a leather cover and a rawhide strap looped around it to keep it closed. It was thicker and heavier than she expected, dense. Harper unwound the cover strap and inhaled its old paper smell.

This was Sofie's diary.

This was the olden days right here.

Harper sat up straight. She rubbed her fingers together and opened the diary carefully. Its spine was stiff with age and gave a faint dry *crick* as it opened. The first page had a childish drawing in pencil of a cabin on it. Harper recognized the picture from the printed version of the diary. The cabin was surrounded by trees and had a thin smokestack pipe sticking out of its roof, with swirly smoke lines rising out of the pipe. Tall, pointy trees surrounded the cabin on both sides, and the ground was littered with huge pinecones.

Here and there, eyes peered out from the shadowy spaces between the trees.

Were they human eyes or animal eyes?

Harper had never noticed it on the printed version of the diary, but the picture, in regular pencil, was kind of creepy. She turned the page and there it was, Sofie's first diary entry from way back in 1860.

March 12th, 1860
Dear Diary,

Hello, I am Sofie! Mama gave you to me because she thinks I talk too much. I think she was jesting but perhaps not.

We shall be great friends, little diary. I shall tell you everything and practice my script. Nobody will read you but me, not even Gerta. You will be my secret!

Yours,
Sofie

Harper smiled. Sofie's handwriting was clear and loopy and totally Sofie. It was as if she'd left part of herself in the pencil lead. Harper turned the diary's pages, scanning the snatches of passages she'd basically memorized. She thumbed all the way to the back of the diary, prepared to start again at the beginning and go more slowly, when she noticed sentences she didn't recognize.

No.

Entire *entries* she didn't recognize.

Harper looked up and surveyed the reading room. Dust motes floated all around her, illuminated by slanting rays of sunlight.

It went further.

The real diary went further.

23

July 26th, 1866
Dear Diary,

Today Gerta and I helped mother with the laundry. It was too hot to work inside the cabin so we went down to the river and washed the clothes on the shoreline, as we did when we were crossing the prairie. When the clothes had enough battering we brought them home and strung them on a line of rope between the trees to dry.

When the wind picked up they fluttered like they still had people inside them. I felt an urge to grab Papa's shirt by its cuffs and twirl around with it for a little dance.

Yours,
    Sofie

July 27th, 1866
Dear Diary,

Last night I dreamt I was floating on the Tender Heart River. I was floating by myself with my toes stiff and pointed toward the sky. The sky was dark and churning and I felt a loneliness creep into my bones. I had never felt so lonely, like a baby bird that's fallen from its nest.

I floated and floated until I was beneath the

mountains and everything was black as pitch. I realized I was dead and there was no way out. The river had ceased moving. The whole world was stopped in hard amber.

Yours,
    Sofie

July 28th, 1866
Dear Diary,

I was in the woods today and saw Everest Hahn huffing with excitement. He'd found a horse standing outside the entrance to a cave. I made him take me to see it. I could hardly believe my eyes but it was the outlaw Crack Donegan's horse, still alive after three years gone wild.

The horse was near starved to death. It had a nasty wound on its right flank, as if some fierce animal had attacked it. I tried to befriend the horse and bring it back to town but it reared up and nearly struck me with its hooves. It wanted nothing to do with us that was plain so we left it to guarding its cave.

Yours,
    Sofie

July 29th, 1866
Dear Diary,

I slept poorly all night long. I kept waking

and picturing Crack Donegan's poor horse alone in front of that cave. With Mr. Donegan so long in the ground it has no one to care for it or to treat its ugly wound. The horse has been raised and taught by human hands but it's now alone in the world.

I think I will return to the cave today and try again to lure the horse back to town. I think it would make Mr. Donegan happy to know his horse has not been lost forever. That it has found a new home.

Yours,
Sofie

Harper stared at the diary's final page, trying to will additional words into existence. Instead of answering any of her questions, the new entries had only increased her curiosity and given her more questions about what had happened to Sofie Helle. Had she rescued Crack Donegan's horse or not? Why hadn't she written more in her diary?

"Find anything interesting?"

Harper looked up. The librarian was standing on the other side of the reading table, smiling at her through his bushy gray beard. The light had shifted in the reading room since she'd entered, slanting in through the high windows and making all the dust motes sparkle. Harper tapped the diary with her finger.

"Have you read this all the way through?"

"Yes, but it was a long time ago."

"There's four entries in here they didn't publish in the book we read for school."

The librarian frowned.

"Really? That's strange."

Harper pushed her chair back and stood up. "I wonder why they left them out."

The librarian reached across the table and turned the diary in his direction. "An editorial error, perhaps," the librarian said, frowning. "A lapse on the publisher's part."

"Maybe. Maybe not." Harper picked the diary up off the table and slipped it back into its special plastic bag. "Okay. I need to make some copies."

"Certainly," the librarian said, gesturing toward a copier machine at the far end of the reading room. "I'm just happy to see a young person so interested in our town's history."

"Oh, it's not history," Harper said, checking her purse for quarters. "This shit is happening right now."

———————

Harper left the library with her freshly copied pages of Sofie's diary and drove downtown. She couldn't tell if it was the large white mocha she'd had earlier or the old-school thrill of trying to solve a mystery, but she felt as if she'd been plugged into an electrical outlet. Something bad had happened to Sofie Helle and she was going to find out what. First she'd been visited by Sofie's ghost the night before, and now these extra diary entries? It couldn't be a coincidence. No way.

Harper parked outside the Emerald Dragon and went inside. The Chinese restaurant was half empty, and Harper could tell in one glance that Eva hadn't shown up yet, which was typical Eva. Harper said hello as a waitress walked across the restaurant to greet her and asked for a booth at the back where she could watch the fish tank. She loved the Dragon's fish tank. It was filled with chubby, sleepy-looking goldfish and dozens of tiny darting fish that glowed purple and yellow in the tank's LED lights. The tank's floor was covered with blue aquarium rocks and had two bubbling treasure chests, their lids eternally flipping open and shut, and one big windmill in the center of the tank that was always turning slowly, giving the fish something to dart through.

The waitress brought two ice waters and a pot of tea with two small porcelain teacups. Harper poured her own cup of tea and stared across the restaurant, taking a breath and trying to center herself.

Find me, Sofie had said.

Find me.

Harper's phone buzzed inside her purse. She took it out, expecting to see a text from Eva about how she was late, but it was actually a call from The Mom. Harper debated declining the call outright but decided she really didn't have anything better to do at the moment.

"Hello?"

"Hi, sweetie. Where are you right now?"

"At the Emerald Dragon. I'm having lunch with Eva."

"Ah. Well, I was just thinking of you and thought I'd check in."

"Thinking of me?"

"Everybody asked about you at church this morning."

Harper's gaze drifted across the restaurant and over to the fish tank. A curious goldfish seemed to be watching her as it nibbled at the tank's glass wall, its fishy cheeks puffed out.

"That's nice," Harper said.

"I said a prayer for you."

"That's double nice."

"It was a prayer of protection and love. Now you have an angel on your shoulder looking out for you."

"So that's what that feeling was. I thought I had a stalker or something."

"Ha ha, very funny. You're such a comedian, Harper."

Harper took a sip of tea.

"All right," The Mom said. "I better go. I want to get some painting done before we start making dinner."

"Okay. See ya."

"Don't eat too much, Harper. We're having spare ribs tonight."

"I won't. Bye."

Harper ended the call and sat back in the booth. A prayer of protection and love. Geez. What a sap The Mom was.

———————

Eva rolled in five minutes later, wearing her sunglasses inside the restaurant like she was a movie starlet. Harper waited, enjoying how lost her friend looked in the dimly lit room, and finally shouted "Hey" and waved her over. Eva sat down, and a gust of blueberry-scented perfume filled the booth.

"Whoa," Harper said. "You wearing enough perfume for lunch?"

Eva took off her sunglasses and threw shade at Harper.

"One of us needs to represent. You look like you just stepped out of a tornado. Have you looked in a mirror today?"

"Thanks. I didn't sleep much."

"Why not? You crushing on somebody?"

The waitress appeared and took their order. When she left, Harper told Eva about the late-night visit from Sofie Helle's ghost and her visit to the library. She took the photocopied pages of Sofie's diary out of her purse and handed them to Eva, who read them while eating three spring rolls, one after the other.

"Something went down at that cave," Eva said when she finished reading the last diary entry. "Sofie should never have gone back."

"You think so?"

Eva nodded. "Why else would she stop writing in her diary? The girl was addicted to writing about herself. She was a little house on the blogger."

"What do you think happened to her?"

Eva shrugged.

"Could have been a bear attack."

"A bear attack?"

"Or wolves. They snatched that Hawthorn baby, right?"

Eva sat back against the booth and sipped her Coke. Her nose and forehead scrunched together as she made her thinking face. "You know, Harp, my tia Maria Elena is always saying Hawthorn is haunted. The whole town. She says white people must have showed up here back in the day and massacred some Indians and then buried their bodies all over the place."

"But they didn't. Nobody lived here until the founders arrived. This area was uninhabited."

"How do you know that? From your Norwegian girlfriend's diary?"

Harper rolled her eyes.

"Eva, you think everything's a conspiracy."

"No, I just think there are some things you can't explain," Eva said, glancing over her shoulder. "Especially when you're getting late-night visits from a dead pioneer girl."

The waitress brought their food, and they dug in. They both had sesame chicken with broccoli and fried rice, the Dragon's best dish by far. Harper felt her jangling nerves calm as she ate, and she let herself space out for a minute. She watched the goldfish drift through crowds of tiny purple and silver fish, apparently content in their endless swimming and not haunted by anything at all.

"I bet she's lonely," Eva said, pointing at Harper with her fork. "Wherever Sofie is, she's probably super lonesome."

"I guess so."

"What do you mean, you guess so? This chick went to all the trouble to track you down and show up in your damn bedroom. That's, like, stalker-level lonely right there."

"I don't know," Harper said. "I think death will be peaceful. Nobody bugs you when you're dead. Nobody expects anything from you."

Eva stared at her. "Damn, Harper. You're really are a hard-core loner, aren't you? I bet you wouldn't mind being thrown in solitary for a few months."

"Would I still get to go for a run every day?"

Eva broke out her trademark mega-loud laugh, and everyone in the restaurant glanced in their direction. Harper felt her purse vibrate against her hip and took out her phone. She'd gotten a text from . . . Olav Helle?

Hi Harper. Are you still interested in Sofie?

Harper glanced across the table. Eva was checking her own phone.

Yes I am Harper texted back.

Cool. I think I know where her body is.

Harper took a quick breath and held it in.

Really?

Yes. Meet me at Brodigan Park at 3:30. I'll show you where she is.

"Who is it, Harp?" Eva said. "Somebody from school?"

Harper licked her lips. This couldn't be a coincidence. No way.

Okay. I'll be there.

"Hellooo? Earth to Harp."

Harper held her phone out to Eva so she could read the texts.

"Huh," Eva said, reclining against the booth. "This girl must really want to meet you."

Harper sat back and crossed her arms.

"But why me?"

Eva tilted her head, puzzled.

"I mean, out of everybody in town. Why did she visit me?"

Eva grinned, her dark eyes gleaming. "Because, Harp. You're always on the lookout. Everybody knows that."

24

WHEN OLAV RETURNED from the Clearing, he brought the shovel and the duffle bag with the skull's remains in it to his car and set them both in the trunk. He was hungry and thirsty and covered in dirt. He leaned into the trunk and unzipped the duffle bag a few inches so he could see the skull's eye sockets.

"So where's the Doorway? Up in the mountains?"

No, the skull said. *The Doorway is southeast from this point. It is down in the valley.*

Olav pulled out his phone and thought a moment. What would get Harper Spurling to go into the valley with him without making her suspicious? They hadn't seen each other since the night he'd killed the moth.

The girl. Tell her you've found the girl.

Olav squinted.

"Sofie?"

Yes.

Olav rubbed his sore neck. He still didn't get the whole Sofie thing, but it was worth a shot, he supposed. What else could he say? Hi, remember me, the dude you hate now? Want to go for a nature hike?

Olav sent the text. Harper replied, almost immediately, and suddenly they had a date in one hour at Brodigan Park, which was a half mile south of Olav's house and also bordered the forest. It was a perfect spot to enter the valley, and remote enough that nobody would notice when two people arrived and only one person left.

This will be your final and greatest kill.

Olav slid his phone back into his pocket. He stared at the skull peeking out at him from the opening in the duffle bag for a long moment and zipped the bag up again. He walked into the front porch of his house, took off his boots, and went inside the house, not even registering the porch's roadkill stink as he passed through. His parents were in the kitchen. His father was drinking beer and reading the Sunday paper while his mother fried something up in a skillet.

Olav's mother looked at him as he entered the room, her eyes bleary from a lack of sleep. One of the other nurses at Burbling Brook had quit suddenly, and his mother had been working extra shifts to help cover for her absence.

"Well, there you are. We thought you were still sleeping."

Olav approached the stove and glanced into the skillet. She was making a grilled ham-and-cheese sandwich.

"You're filthy," his mother said, frowning. "What did you do, wake up early and decide to find out how much dirt you could roll around in?"

"I was treasure hunting in the woods. Can I have a sandwich?"

"Treasure hunting?" his father said, lowering the sports page. "In these woods?"

Olav shrugged and got a glass out of the cupboard. He ran the tap and stuck his finger under it, waiting for the water to grow cold before he filled the glass and chugged it.

"You never know," he said, burping and filling the glass a second time.

"Yes, you do," his father said, snorting. "Ain't shit in there but trees and critters that want to kill you or eat you after something else kills you."

"That's not true," his mother said. "There's deer and they're as sweet as it gets."

His father laughed, and Olav knew what he was going to say before he said it.

"Deer are the worst bastards of all. They'll kill you on the highway without even trying. I scraped up seven this week, every one of them covered in broken glass with chunks of plastic and metal littered everywhere."

"But that's our fault, for driving too fast," his mother said, scooping the grilled sandwich off the skillet with a spatula and putting it on a plate. She handed the plate to Olav and winked. "There you go, sweetie."

"Hey," his father said, taking a swig of beer. "That was supposed to be my sandwich."

"Sorry, pal. He looked hungrier."

"Well, shit."

Olav's mother patted Olav's cheek.

"You're still my baby boy, you know that?"

Olav nodded. He knew he was supposed to feel something when his mother talked like this, that she was being sentimental and loving, but he really didn't feel anything but glad she didn't suspect him of anything, even though he was covered in dirt and had been gone for hours. It'd been like this for as long as he could remember, with both his parents and other adults. He learned what he needed from them, watched them warily, and felt nothing but a remote gladness when they let him sail past them without questioning him too closely.

"That sandwich sure smells good," his father said.

"Oh, hush," Olav's mother said, slapping together another sandwich from supplies on the counter. Olav left the room, taking his lunch with him to his bedroom. He ate at his desk and then took a shower, scrubbing off all the dirt and shampooing his hair. He wanted to look normal for Harper, and the shower felt good on his back and arms, which ached from all the digging. He got out of the shower, dried off, put on deodorant, and combed his hair. He felt excited and full of energy, just like he had the afternoon before Kira Fredrickson's hot tub party.

Man, Kira Fredrickson.

Sitting alone in the hot tub in her bikini one minute . . .

Floating face down in it another.

Olav shivered. He had an erection, but he didn't have time to do anything about it other than shove it down into his underwear and jeans and wait for the ache to go away. He put on a clean T-shirt and a flannel jacket and fresh socks. He pulled the cigar box down from the shelf in his closet and looked over his six kill trophies. He picked up Kira's wine cooler cap and rubbed it between his fingers. Something like peace filled his mind, pushing away the buzzing that was always there, droning on and on like background music. He kissed the wine cooler cap, set it back in the cigar box, and set the box back on his shelf. He grabbed his keys, phone, and wallet and walked back through the house.

His parents had finished eating lunch and moved to the living room. His father was sprawled out on the sofa, snoring lightly, and his mother was flipping through a magazine while watching some kind of travel show. She'd always talked about going to France one day, but they never had enough money for that. They'd never even gone to California.

"You're going out again?"

"Yep," Olav said.

His mother looked up at him.

"You look nice. Got a hot date?"

"Maybe."

"Anyone I know?"

"No."

"Uh huh," his mother said, looking back down at her magazine again and flipping a page. "Just remember: always be a gentleman."

"Yes, ma'am."

Olav walked through the kitchen and went out to the front porch to put on his boots. This time he did notice the roadkill stench, but it didn't bother him much. It smelled like work.

———

Olav arrived at Brodigan Park ten minutes early. The park, which was currently empty, had a playground and a plaque for Mary Sheila Brodigan, a rich old lady who'd donated the money to build it back in the sixties. Olav got the duffle bag and shovel out of the trunk, carried them through the park, and set them at the foot of the trail leading down to the valley. He took out his pack of cigarettes and sat down on a bench with a good view of the parking lot.

What does the day look like?

"Huh?"

Through your eyes. Through the eyes of the living.

Olav pulled his lighter out of his pocket and lit the cigarette. He liked this park, he remembered. He'd come here when he was younger with his mother, and she'd pushed him on the swings until he went up so high he thought he'd flip through the atmosphere and sail into the sun. Even back then, it had taken something extreme to really rattle his cage.

"It's nice," Olav said, looking around. "It's sunny, only a couple of clouds. I can smell somebody grilling burgers."

And how does it feel to be young?

Olav coughed into his hand, his throat catching on the cigarette smoke.

"Good, I guess."

When I was young, I walked across plains covered in lush grass, and the sun was warm on my face. Clouds floated above me like cottonseed, darkening with rain when the world needed rain. I bathed in hot springs, and the wind dried my skin. There were great beasts to hunt, and I had a strong woman to hunt with. At night we would sleep beneath the stars wrapped in many animal skins. We had many strong children.

Olav exhaled.

"That sounds pretty good."

Then came the great fires. The great beasts died out, and we grew hungry. We warred amongst ourselves, without mercy, until bloodlust and victory were the only things we cared for. Entire tribes were wiped out until only the strongest tribe remained. This tribe, my tribe, had learned to do many things. The world was still young and rife with magic. We could send our spirits out of our bodies and soaring across the land. We could send our spirits to the stars and feed on the solar winds. Each of us lived for centuries, sometimes millennia. We dug under the mountains and created a kingdom below to match our kingdom above.

A green jeep pulled into the parking lot. Olav squinted, trying to make out the figures inside. It was Harper and another girl. Eva Alvarez.

Shit. He hadn't counted on a second person.

But then came a sweeping blood thirst and we fell upon ourselves. Those who survived retreated underground.

"But you didn't make it."

No, I did not. But I will today. I will be the last to straggle home, and you will be the one to bring me there.

Olav stood up and waved to Harper. She waved back at him, and the two girls talked for a few seconds before getting out of the jeep and heading in his direction. Olav took a final drag on his cigarette and dropped it on the ground, grinding it out beneath his boot. This would mean two more kills . . .

Well.

Eight was a symmetrical number, wasn't it? It was basically the sign for infinity, standing upright.

The Doorway
(1866)

Sofie Helle slept fitfully and woke alone in her family's cabin. It was midmorning, and she'd slept through breakfast. She'd dreamed all night of Crack Donegan's starving, wounded horse as it stood suffering outside the hillside cave. How had the horse survived for three years on its own? What exactly had attacked it?

Sofie got dressed, drank a cup of water, and ate an apple and cheese for breakfast. She retrieved her diary and pencil from beneath her mattress and went outside to sit in her father's smoking chair. She sharpened the pencil with her father's whittling knife, which he kept beside the chair in a tin can. She closed her eyes and turned her face to the sun.

The cave.

What was in that cave?

Sofie itched her nose and wrote in her diary. When she finished writing, she went back inside the cabin, set the diary and pencil on the table, and gathered a handful of carrots in a basket. Even the most cantankerous horses loved carrots.

Sofie walked into the forest on the east side of Hawthorn and made her way down into the valley, grabbing at trees and rocks to help slow her down on the steeper parts. The sun was already warming the world, and the air smelled like pine needles baking in the light. Squirrels leapt from branch to branch above her head in the forest canopy, chittering at each other. When she reached the valley floor, Sofie looked to the western ridgeline to get her bearings. This was the spot where she'd encountered Everest Hahn. She remembered hiking south for perhaps a mile along the valley floor before they'd come to the cave, which was tucked beneath an outcropping of rock that had reminded her of a cloud bank. She started retracing this route, watching the ridgeline for guidance.

The forest grew quieter and the sound of songbirds stopped altogether. Sofie became worried she'd already passed the cave, but then there it was, tucked in beneath the cloud bank formation in the valley wall. She stepped out of the trees and approached the cave, every sound loud and unnaturally magnified in her ears.

Crack Donegan's horse was lying on the ground in front of the cave. Sofie could tell immediately that it was dead. Flies swarmed its carcass, and as Sofie took another step forward she noticed maggots—thousands of maggots—squirming in feasting ecstasy in its open wound. The wind gusted, and the stench it carried her way was worse than anything Sofie had ever smelled before, indescribably foul, and she would have vomited if she'd had a heavier breakfast.

Sofie untied her bonnet and held it over her face. The eye-watering stench was like a wall pushing back at her, but she continued forward anyway, carefully stepping around the dead horse and stopping at the cave's entrance.

"Hello?" Sofie called out. "Is anyone back there?"

No one answered her, of course. Sofie blushed at her own timidity. Why would anybody be in this cave? What had she expected to find here? One of the wicked trolls from the old country? She was being ridiculous.

Sofie took a breath through the fabric of her bonnet and entered the cave, still carrying her basket of carrots. It was cool and dim, but she could make out a pocket of light up ahead. She kept walking, following the cave's serpentine curves, for what seemed like a long, long time. She reached a puddle of light and looked up—a small shaft in the rock went straight up some twenty feet to what must have been the surface. A few yards past the puddle of light, the tunnel ended and a doorway appeared. The doorway had been carved out of the cave's rocky floor and was set at a sharp slant, leading to a descending flight of roughly hewn stairs.

A cold wind gusted up from below, smelling like water and minerals. This must have been an old mining tunnel, she realized. This tunnel led to a larger space.

"Hello?"

The wind died down and was replaced by a profound silence. Sofie could hear her own heart lub-lubbing in her chest. She placed a tentative foot on the first step beyond the doorway. Nothing happened, so she took another step, and then another. She felt as if she were entering the heart of the earth. She continued farther down the stairs until the doorway was high above her and she could see more pools of light in the far distance below.

"Hello? Is anyone down there?"

A loud thud came from somewhere above the tunnel's ceiling, and loosened dirt fell upon her. Sofie's skin rippled with gooseflesh.

She should not have come here.

Not alone.

Not ever.

Another thud came from overhead, much louder than the first. It sounded like . . . blasting. Like dynamite blasting.

"Oh," Sofie said, looking back up the stairs. She'd taken only three return steps up the stairway before a third thud, loudest of all, shook the tunnel like an earthquake and the small doorway she'd come through only a minute before disappeared before her eyes, obscured by a large slide of rock.

Oh, Lord.

She was trapped.

Sofie clutched the owl charm on her necklace and said a prayer to the spirit of Crack Donegan. She also prayed to God and to her mother and father. To anything or anyone who might have been watching. Who could sense her peril.

The world remained silent.

Days went past.

No one could hear the trapped girl, pounding for help from beneath the earth.

Eventually, she stopped pounding.

25

AS THEY DROVE from the Emerald Dragon to Brodigan Park, Harper found herself thinking about Josh Keegan's mom. How she'd just been sitting on her couch in the dark, surrounded by empty wine bottles. How sad she'd been. How certain she'd been that Josh was innocent.

He didn't do it.

He loved her more than anything.

Okay, say Mrs. Keegan was right. Who had killed Kira Fredrickson, then? Who would even have known about the cabin up in the mountains? If it had been the Tender Heart Killer, Kira's was a different kind of murder. The Tender Heart Killer's other victims had all been found washed up on the riverbank in town, not left wherever they'd been killed. Why would the Tender Heart Killer have deviated from his normal procedure?

Maybe Kira wasn't a normal victim for the Tender Heart Killer.

Maybe he knew her.

Personally.

"Holy shit," Harper said.

Eva glanced up from her cell phone.

"Huh?"

Harper swallowed and squeezed the steering wheel.

"What if the Tender Heart Killer isn't some random older guy? What if he's somebody our age?"

Eva laughed.

"You mean somebody from school?"

"Maybe."

Eva snorted and resumed texting on her phone. "Right. One of the goofballs from Hawthorn High has managed to kill five people and avoid the cops this whole time. Good one, Sherlock."

"Seriously. What if the killer knew Kira? What if he knew she'd be up at her cabin without her parents?"

"You mean like Josh?"

"No. The real killer. Shit. Maybe he was at the hot tub party the night before. Do you even know all those guys who were sitting around the campfire? The seniors and juniors?"

Eva rolled her eyes.

"Oh yeah. All those hippy stoners looked real dangerous."

They arrived at Brodigan Park, and Harper parked on the street. Olav Helle, dressed in blue jeans and a gray hoodie, was sitting on a bench at the rear of the small park. He stood up and waved in their direction. Harper waved back and unbuckled her seat belt.

"You know what?" Eva said, finally stashing her phone in her pocket. "Olav Helle's kind of cute when you think about it."

"Yeah, right."

Eva eyed her.

"Holy shit. You still like him."

"No I don't."

"Ha, you so do."

Eva puckered her lips and blew Harper air kisses. Harper blushed and glanced at Olav.

"Stop it. He's watching."

"Oh, no. The boy is watching!"

"Let's just get this over with," Harper said, opening her door and getting out of the car. Eva followed her, and they entered the park. They passed the playground equipment, which they'd both spent many happy hours on when they were little, and joined Olav by his bench. Harper smelled cigarette smoke and remembered Olav liked to smoke, even in his car. Who still smoked in their own car?

"Hi," Olav said.

"Hey," Harper said.

"Oooh," Eva said. "I am feeling the tension here, people."

Harper scowled at her friend. Eva primped her hair and gave her a wide troublemaker smile. She was loving this.

"You said you know where Sofie is?"

Olav nodded, maintaining eye contact with Harper in that serious way he always did, as if you were in a staring contest with him. He was so freaking intense.

"I asked my grandpa about her. He said she disappeared into one of the caves down in the valley and no one ever saw her again."

"Did you say caves?" Eva said. "You think we're going spelunking?"

"You don't have to," Olav said. "But I am. I know which cave it is. My grandpa showed me."

Harper eyed the duffle bag and the shovel lying on the ground beside the bench.

"So those are, like, your cave tools?"

"Yeah. They should be all we need."

Harper looked at Eva. Her friend shrugged and took out her cell phone to check it.

"It's up to you, lady. You're the one being haunted."

Olav angled his head, his eyes somehow growing a notch bluer.

"Haunted?"

Harper peered at the woods behind Olav. "Sofie's ghost visited me last night. She told me to find her."

Olav looked down at the duffle bag. He seemed surprised.

"Well," Eva said, texting on her phone, "we gonna do this business or what? I've got shit to do."

Harper studied Olav. She remembered the look on his face as he'd ripped apart the moth on her back patio, but she also remembered him in the hot tub at Kira Fredrickson's party, content as he floated in the bubbling water and watched the starry night sky. She'd liked that Olav. She'd liked that Olav a lot.

"Okay," Harper said, "lead the way."

———

They followed Olav down the park's rocky trail to the valley floor. Harper had played in the park a hundred times as a kid, but the valley path seemed different to her now.

The forest was quiet. Everything was muffled, and the few birdcalls she heard seemed to come from a long way off. The forest floor was also surprisingly dark for the middle of the afternoon. All the trees, fighting for space thirty feet off the ground, blotted out the sky.

They went south through the woods, sticking close to the eastern valley wall. Harper studied the back of Olav's head, wondering what he was thinking. Wondering what she was thinking.

"This is a real live adventure," Eva said, taking a joint out of her purse and lighting it. "Like we're in a fairy tale."

Harper glanced at the shovel head on Olav's shoulder and the duffle bag he was carrying. What exactly was cave stuff, anyhow? A bunch of flashlights? Some rope? Was he going to dig his way into the cave?

Olav muttered something without turning to look back at them. Was he talking to himself?

Eva passed the joint, and Harper took a deep drag. She let the smoke seep into her bloodstream and calm her nerves. They kept walking until Olav turned right suddenly and led them out of the tree line. The valley's limestone cliff rose up before them, too steep to climb. A small oval-shaped cave lay at the base of the cliff, hardly big enough for one person to enter. They halted outside its entrance and peered into the darkness beyond. Olav mumbled to himself again and Eva and Harper looked at each other, eyebrows raised.

"You okay there, Olav?" Eva said. "You seeing a ghost?"

"This is it," Olav said, turning to look at them. "Sofie's somewhere in there."

"You have any flashlights in that bag?"

Olav shook his head.

"No. But I've got a flashlight app on my phone."

"Oh yeah," Harper said. "I guess we all do."

Eva took a last drag on her joint and stomped it out. They lit up their cell phone flashlights and entered the cave, which was wide at first but began to narrow as it wound back and forth and terminated, finally, at a pile of loose rock.

Olav set his duffle bag down and started pulling off the bigger rocks and rolling them away from the pile. Harper and Eva held back, watching their feet. "Look at the boy," Eva said, grinning as she nudged Harper in the side. "He's working up a sweat."

"Let him work," Harper said, frowning. "I'm good right here."

Harper checked her phone, but she didn't get any reception in the cave. She wondered what The Mom and everybody else was currently up to—it'd be time for dinner soon, and unexplained dinner absences were frowned on. What were they having again? Ribs?

Olav finally got the bigger rocks cleared away, grunting like a real manly-man and using the shovel when he needed leverage, and eventually an outline of a doorway appeared. It was slanted downward, like the entrance to a tornado shelter, and as Olav dug out the last of the major rocks, a set of stone steps appeared, leading downward. A strong, chilly wind blew through the doorway, carrying with it the sense of an enormous space beyond.

"Whoa," Eva said. "That actually leads somewhere."

Harper put her hand on Olav's shoulder. "How'd you know this entrance would be here, Olav? Did your grandpa show you this?"

"Not exactly," Olav said, shrugging off her hand and ducking through the doorway. Something hard in his voice made Harper's stomach twist. Actually, her stomach had been twisting ever since she'd received his text. Why was he being so helpful about finding Sofie Helle? What was in all this for him? Was he just trying to impress her and make up for the moth? Or was something else on his mind?

"I don't know about this," Harper said, looking back at Eva. "What if the entrance collapses while we're in there?"

Olav went down the first couple of steps and turned back around. He held her gaze, all calm and serious. As if all this was inevitable.

"She's down there, Harper. She's waiting for us."

"This is an adventure, Harp," Eva said, reaching out and squeezing her hand. "Adventures get risky."

"I guess so."

Harper looked back at the doorway and Olav's shadowed outline.

"She visited you, Harp," Eva said. "You said it yourself."

Harper nodded and took a deep breath.

Find me.

"Right. Let's go."

Harper and Eva followed Olav through the doorway while using their cell phones to make out the steps. It was a tunnel with stairs cut into the rocky floor. The stairs were narrow, and the tunnel roof was low enough that Olav and Harper had to duck their heads.

"This must have been an old mine entrance," Harper said. "Sofie wrote about the Dennison Mining Company blasting near town."

They went down and down. The air grew colder, and the stairs were slick with moisture. Eventually the tunnel ended at another doorway and they emerged into a vast cavern. "Holy crap," Harper said. She swung her head from left to right, trying to take it all in. Three rough holes perforated the cavern's shadowy ceiling, arranged in a formation that resembled two empty eye sockets and a round, screaming mouth. The holes let in a limited amount of sunlight, but the cavern was so large much of its open space remained murky, as if it were filled with smoke.

Harper made out the chalky white outline of a winding, open stone drain carved along the cavern's walls. The elaborate drain started high up and wound all the way around the cavern several times in a corkscrew pattern, terminating at the back of the cavern and pouring out into a narrow waterfall.

"Jesus Mary," Eva said. "This place is mammoth."

Olav kept walking straight ahead toward the waterfall, and Eva wandered off to look at something. Harper remained outside the entrance to the tunnel stairway for a minute, still taking the whole scene in. This was like a small world carved inside the world she'd always known, like in *A Journey to the Center of the Earth*.

Something moved on the ceiling. It was small and fluttery . . .

Bats.

Of course the cavern's ceiling was covered in a million bats. This was basically the fucking Bat Cave—

"Harp!"

Harper turned to her left and saw Eva fifty feet away, her features illuminated by her cell phone's light.

"Come over here. You should see this."

Harper walked over to her friend, who was holding her cell phone beneath her chin to illuminate her face.

"Check this out." Eva shone her phone's light across the floor of the cave, which was sprinkled with chunks of rock that sparkled in a way that made Harper's breath catch in her throat.

"Remember geology in middle school?"

Harper knelt and picked up a rock that was shaped like a chisel. It was nearly clear, with a patch of frosted white at its base and a sharp, pointed end.

"It's quartz, right?"

"Yeah. I think so."

Eva laughed and picked up a rock herself. "All these babies could be worth something. They might be precious. Or semiprecious."

Harper smiled and slipped the chisel-shaped fragment into her back pocket. Maybe this was what Sofie had been doing down here. Maybe she was hunting for treasure.

Eva picked up more chunks of quartz until her arms were full.

"We're going to need a couple of bags—"

A loud clang rang out, and Eva pitched face-first onto the ground, the rocks she'd been holding dropping from her arms and thudding back onto the cavern floor. Olav, who must have put down the duffle bag and circled behind them, stepped out of the murky shadows holding his shovel. He grinned.

It was Olav, Harper realized, her stomach twisting into an even tighter knot.

Olav Helle was the Tender Heart Killer.

26

HARPER KNELT OVER her friend without dropping her gaze from Olav. Eva was out cold, but she was still breathing, her chest rising and falling in shallow inhalations. Olav patted his palm on the shovel's handle, looking pleased with himself, his mouth hooked in an ugly snarl.

"Sorry. You never said you were bringing a friend. I would have warned you about that."

Harper stood up. She looked over Olav's shoulder. The tunnel stairway back to the surface suddenly looked very far off.

"You can try to run," Olav said. "You're a runner, right?"

Harper swallowed and curled her hands into hard little fists.

"Go ahead, Harper. Run."

Harper glanced down at Eva. "She'll stay, though," Olav said, taking a step forward. "She'll stay, and you'll never see her again. And that'll be all because of you."

Harper studied Olav's face. He was serious. He was serious and he was whackadoo crazy. She could see it now, how something was loose behind his bright blue eyes. Harper suddenly thought of The Mom and her prayer of protection. Shit. She loved The Mom so much. She was always just trying to look out for Harper. She was a good mom.

Harper would hug her so tight the next time she saw her. A big-time hug.

"What do you want, Olav?"

Olav set the shovel on his shoulder and nodded behind her. "It's actually what it wants. The skull."

"The skull?"

"Remember? The one I found?"

Harper nodded. Their conversation in the hot tub was all coming back to her now. Including that look in his eyes when everything had changed. When he'd suddenly wanted to bring her home, like something had whispered in his ear.

"So you're the Tender Heart Killer," Harper said. "You killed Kira."

Olav dropped the shovel from his shoulder and pointed it at the waterfall across the cavern. "Let me show you something."

Harper stepped back.

"Uh, no thanks."

Olav looked at Eva on the ground and tightened his grip on the shovel, his entire body tensing. Harper realized that if he got started swinging again, more people were going to die. She needed to keep him going. To talk about his craziness. She needed an opportunity.

"All right. Show me."

Harper turned around and started walking toward the waterfall. She still had her purse slung around her shoulder, and she went over its contents in her mind: lip gloss, wallet, cell phone, keys, tiny Kleenex packet, lighter, tampons, and a mini-bottle of ibuprofen. Not exactly a dangerous weapons arsenal.

"It's not just a skull anymore," Olav said as they approached the waterfall. "I dug up its whole body."

The duffle bag Olav had been carrying appeared on the ground in front of them. Olav knelt down and unzipped it.

"Look."

Olav dumped out the duffle bag and a pile of bones tumbled out, skull and all.

"He was one of them. The Ones Who Built in Darkness."

Harper stared at the bones, trying to process this logic. "The Ones Who Built in Darkness was just a story," she said, "a tall tale Crack Donegan told Sofie."

"The skull was quartered while he was still alive," Olav said, ignoring her reply. "That means his limbs were all hacked off from his torso."

"Jesus."

Harper exhaled and took a deep breath.

"So you, what, talk to it?"

"Sometimes. When it wants to talk. I can hear its voice inside my head. It knows what I'm thinking."

Harper rubbed her eyes. "Maybe you have a brain tumor, Olav. Maybe that's why you're hearing voices."

"No. This is all real." Olav licked his lips. "Sorry."

Harper scowled. Grandma Spurling said the word *sorry* was an asshole's calling card. That if you ever met a boy who had to say sorry to you all the time, you were better off kicking him out of bed and sleeping alone.

"But what's this got to do with me and Eva?"

Olav circled the skeleton and pointed toward the base of the waterfall. Harper came around on the other side of the skeleton and looked down, unsure of what she was looking at. Actually, it was all darkness—she was staring into an enormous pit that went straight down. There was no lake or river at the end of the corkscrewing drain waterfall; just a lot of empty space that made her feel lightheaded.

"They call this the Well," Olav said, peering over the pit's edge. "It's where they're sleeping now."

"Sleeping?"

"They don't die. They just hibernate."

Harper stared into the Well.

"That's from the Tender Heart River," Harper said, nodding at the waterfall. "The river's draining into the Well, isn't it?"

"I think part of it cycles through here," Olav said, squatting down and peering into the pit. "They need to be connected to the aboveground world. They feed on life."

Harper thought she could make out splotches of faint blue light way down in the pit, but that might have been an optical illusion.

Probably most definitely an optical illusion.

"That's why I needed someone," Olav said, standing up again. "The skull can't enter the Well without a human sacrifice."

Harper's throat tightened.

"And you picked me? For the sacrifice?"

Olav shrugged. "I couldn't think of anybody else I could get to come down here. Sorry, Harper."

Harper imagined plummeting into all that darkness.

Sorry, sorry.

Harper turned around and faced Olav. Her legs were quivering with adrenalin just as they did before she burst out of the blocks at a track meet. Every little fraidy-cat nerve in her body told her to run, to run away from this psycho RIGHT NOW, but she took her purse off her shoulder instead and set it beside her on the ground. She set her cell phone on the ground, too, and turned the flashlight app off. She'd been underground long enough. She could see in the cavern's murk.

The skull stared up at her, perched right in the middle of its jumbled body, like a spider in the middle of its web. Harper reached out and ran her finger along the skeleton's ribcage. It felt cool and dry to the touch, though it tingled a little, as if it had more buzzing molecules inside it than a normal object.

"Do you think it hurts to die, Olav?"

Olav came up beside her and loomed over her shoulder. She could smell his shampoo. He must have taken a shower before they met in the park.

"Depends on the way you die, I suppose," Olav said. "Back when I helped my dad with cleanup on the highway, we'd find these animals with their stomachs ripped open who were still crawling, trying to go down the road or back into the forest. Sometimes they wouldn't even have their hind legs anymore."

Harper picked up one of the long arm bones—the humerus?—and tapped it against her palm.

No.

It was too light to make a good weapon. Too fragile.

"My dad always said the animals were dead already, except they didn't know it yet," Olav said. "He had a special club to take them out with. He could usually kill them with one solid hit, but it usually took me a few extra."

"You know what, Olav?" Harper said, tossing the bone back onto the pile and looking Olav straight in the eye. "You're pretty fucked up."

Olav swung the shovel right off the tip of his shoe and smacked Harper beneath the jaw. Suddenly she was lying flat on her back, her head ringing and her mouth filling with blood.

She'd bitten her tongue.

Bad.

"You're such a fucking snotty bitch."

Olav appeared above her, a darker outline against the shadowy cavern ceiling. Now the shovel was raised on his shoulder. Harper sat up and scuttled backward like a crab. Olav stepped forward, grinning and matching her pace. She stopped scuttling.

"Just because you have a nicer house. Just because your parents make more money. You're always watching everybody else. Always judging."

Harper turned her head to the side and spat blood. She could not think of what to do next. How to save herself.

She spat more blood.

Oh fuck.

She was going to die.

"So-fee," Harper said, spitting out more blood (though apparently still capable of speaking). "What about So-fee? Ith she here?"

Olav shook his head. "Are you kidding? You're about to die and you still care about my stupid ancestor? You're the one that's really fucked up, Harper. You can't even live your own life. You have to live through others' lives instead."

The ceiling fluttered beyond Olav as the bats started rustling. Harper took a deep breath and rose up onto her knees. She put her hands behind her back and leaned forward, execution-style. She felt the pointed fragment of quartz in her back pocket and gripped it by its blunt end.

"Okay," she said. "Go ahead, ath-hole. I'm tired of talking to you."

Olav nodded.

"Thank you for your sacrifice, Harper."

Olav raised the shovel above his head, winding up to swing, and as he did, Harper sprang forward and stabbed him as hard as she could with the quartz fragment. Olav groaned as he dropped the shovel and clutched his gut. Already on her feet, Harper picked up the shovel and circled behind him. As he turned toward her, his whole face a snarl, Harper swung the shovel as hard as she could, smacking Olav in the forehead and sending him sprawling into the bones. Harper waited a few seconds, panting from the fight, but he was out cold.

She leaned over his face, checked to see that he was still

breathing, and spat a fresh glob of blood right onto his forehead.

"Fuck you, Olath."

———————

Harper collected her purse and cell phone with shaking hands. She felt like puking, but this was not the time for puking.

No.

This was the time for escaping.

She grabbed Olav's now-empty duffle bag and re-crossed the cavern floor, using the light from Eva's cell phone to guide her back to her friend. Eva was still unconscious but breathing steadily. She picked up Eva's cell phone and shook her shoulder.

"Eva. We need to go."

Eva groaned and turned over.

"Now, Eva. Wake up."

Harper shone the camera's light over the field of quartz rocks lying on the cavern floor. She put a few of the rocks in the duffle bag—they'd need proof that all this shit had really happened—and noticed a different kind of glint about twenty yards distant. A soft, metallic type of glint.

The temperature dropped as if Harper had just stepped into a walk-in freezer, and the little hairs pricked up along the nape of her neck. She picked her way through the quartz rocks and made her way to the source of the metallic glinting. She discovered an entire human skeleton, lying on the ground as if waiting for a forensic anthropologist to study it. The reflective glint she'd noticed had come from a silver necklace resting on its ribcage. Harper, fingers trembling, set the empty duffle bag down beside the skeleton and lifted up the necklace's charm so she could get a better look.

The charm featured an owl with a name engraved beneath it.

Sofie Helle

Harper smiled, her eyes growing damp.
All right.
Now they could all leave.

27

KNOCKED OUT COLD, Olav Helle lay on the cavern floor and dreamed he was a boy living among wolves.

The wolves lay sprawled about outside their den, sleeping uneasily beneath the burning stars. Their legs twitched as they ran in their sleep, their blackened gums pulled back in unconscious sleep snarls. Olav lay curled among them in the high grass, naked except for an animal pelt knotted across his waist. The wolves had claimed him as their own—they shared their kills with him, and their periods of great hunger, and he smelled as rank as any of them. Dried blood had long ago stained his face and hands. His hair was crusted with dirt and flecked with bone.

Olav had learned to howl with the wolves, to run with them. During a hunt, he could sense when the pack was going to move as soon as the muscles in the alpha's back twitched. His legs burned with the joy of running, and his eyes could spot movement for miles. His mouth ached with the killing hunger. His fingers had become claws.

He had forgotten his mother and father.

He had forgotten his own name.

When the night turned from black to dark blue, the other members of the pack stirred and sniffed at the ground. Olav yawned and stretched and felt the night's long fasting ache in his stomach. The alpha shook himself awake, sniffing the cool air, and suddenly the entire pack was on the move, loping after the alpha as they began the morning's hunt. They crossed the plains easily, the mountains a shadow in the corner of their vision. The sun warmed their backs. They stopped, drank along the shore of a small lake, and continued on.

Around midday, the pack came upon an old buffalo who'd fallen away from its herd and was staggering along, pestered by a thick swarm of flies as a buzzard circled lazily above it in the sky. The wolves fell upon the buffalo, but it had more fight left in it than they expected. The buffalo turned and charged into their midst, throwing the wolves off even as they tore chunks of flesh from its tough hide. Olav leapt at the buffalo, hoping to make the kill himself, but it caught him with a sharp horn and tossed him aside into the high grass. The world spun, and the pack continued to attack the buffalo while Olav lay wounded, his hand pressed against his bleeding side. He heard snarling and yelping and finally a deep animal groan as the buffalo dropped to the earth with a heavy thump.

Olav listened to his pack mates feasting on the fallen buffalo—the sound of bones crunching and flesh tearing, low growls as they argued among themselves for the choicest parts—and understood with dream clarity they would be coming for him next, fresh blood dripping from their muzzles.

They could already smell his wound.

His weakness.

It is time.

Ten more minutes, Mom. Please.

Wake. I have waited long enough.

My head hurts.

You must rise.

Olav opened his eyes. His ears rang, but he could hear the roar of water in the distance—his mom or dad must have been taking a shower. He sat up slowly, and pain filled his head, blotting out his vision and replacing everything with fuzzy lights: a fireworks display of pain. He waited the pain out, gripping his head between his hands, and when he could think again he realized he was not at home, that he was not in his bedroom.

No.

He was still in *their* home.

Yes. And now you must stay with us.

Olav rubbed his face and tried to think. His stomach hurt. He touched where it hurt and his hand came away sticky.

The old buffalo had gored him.

No.

Harper Spurling. The fucking bitch had stabbed him.

Rise, Olav Helle.

Olav looked at the skull. It was sitting beside him among the rest of its bones. The cavern was darker than it had been earlier. He must have been out for hours. It would be night soon, and even the little light that filtered down from the cavern's ceiling would be gone. He could only imagine how dark this place got at night.

"I tried," Olav said, his voice croaking as he spoke aloud. "I tried my best."

Yes, but you have failed.

"But—"

The other living have departed, so it must be you, Olav Helle.

"No."

Olav pushed himself off the ground and wavered uncertainly on his feet. He pressed his hand to his stomach and felt more wetness running through his fingers. His blood. He was bleeding, and Harper Spurling had stabbed him. Just like that, she'd stabbed him. Fuck.

Olav looked past the skull and toward the cavern's stone staircase. It seemed so far away.

Olav took a few more painful steps. More floating lights passed through his vision, and the shadows around him seemed to swirl and consolidate. They almost looked like . . . human shapes, shuffling toward him.

The skull chuckled softly.

You don't recognize them, mighty hunter? They know you. They would know you with their eyes ripped out and their noses sewn shut.

Olav blinked and took a step back.

No.

They were dead.

All of them were dead.

The line between death and life is thinner near the Well, the skull said. *It is your time to cross it.*

Six human shapes, and now he could make out their features, though they still seemed to be made of nothing but shadow. It was the crying old lady. The hunter. The pervert businessman. The lady jogger. The fishing kid.

And, of course, Kira Fredrickson.

"Leave me alone."

The shadows stepped closer. Olav noticed a seventh, smaller shadow entwining itself at their feet, rubbing up against their shadow legs.

It was the neighbors' cat.

Cooper.

"None of you are real," Olav said, raising his hands. "None of this is real."

The skull chuckled again, and the sound was louder this time, like thunder bouncing off the hills. Olav retreated farther as the shadows advanced. He knew that if they touched him they would steal his soul, and that would be worse than death. That would trap him forever and leave him at their mercy. Their touch would be like frostbite, and he would never get warm again, no matter how close to a fire he stood.

The roaring grew louder. He'd come up against the edge of the Well. The waterfall was at his back now, and the encroaching shadows had him surrounded on all sides.

"Sorry I killed you," Olav said to the shadows, squaring his shoulders. "But you can't have me."

The shadows paused, their faces wavering in the dim light.

Death is not the end, the skull said.

"It isn't?"

No, Olav. Not for you.

Olav swallowed. He thought about his parents getting ready to sit down to Sunday dinner and wondered if they'd miss him. What would they think when they found the cigar box of kill trophies in his closet? Would they be surprised? *Totally* surprised? Or would they realize they weren't that surprised at all, actually, that they'd always sensed something off about their only child? Something wrong? Something . . . blank?

Olav Helle turned around, contemplated the continuously plummeting water, and leapt into the abyss.

It went on for a long time.

The Girl Who Was Buried at Last

Five days later, on a fine summer day, the town of Hawthorn buried the pioneer girl named Sofie Helle.

They placed Sofie's bones between her parents in the oldest section of the Hawthorn cemetery and gave her a full graveside service. Harper Spurling was there. So were The Mom and The Dad. Grandma Spurling was there. The Brothers were there, dressed in stiff new clothes and kicking each other in the shins when they thought nobody was looking. Mrs. Randolph, the high school history teacher, was there. Eva Alvarez, her head still bandaged, was there. Josh Keegan, freshly released from jail, was also there, looking relieved with his exhausted parents by his side. In fact, most of Hawthorn was in attendance, dressed in funeral black and eager to witness local history.

Pastor Knutson from the Hawthorn Lutheran church performed the brief burial service. When it was over, Harper turned in her folding chair and studied the crowd. For a moment she didn't see living people, with living flesh on their bones and lungs filled with air. She saw only skeletons—hundreds of vulnerable, lonesome skeletons—rising to their feet, and she felt her heart squeeze as they dispersed across the grassy cemetery lawn.

"You've done good, kid," Grandma Spurling said, hooking Harper's elbow with her own. "Now let's get some lunch."

"Okay, Gram."

They walked back through the graveyard together. Harper raised her face to the cloudless blue sky, basking in the sun's warm light. She could feel the muted presence of Jamie Stendhal, Kira Fredrickson, and all the other people Olav Helle had killed—they were finally at peace, and he was gone. She could hear her parents talking with each other in low, comfortable voices and her little brothers laughing as they ran among the graves. She could feel a warm wind sweep through the trees, blown in from the open prairie.

This, Harper Spurling thought.

This moment right now.

Acknowledgments

I would like to thank my agent, Jonathan Lyons, who read several versions of this novel and offered helpful insight, as always. I would also like to thank the industrious staff at Flux, including my editor Mari Kesselring, publicist Megan Naidl, and book designer Jake Nordby.

Much thanks and gratitude to my family and friends, including Jennifer Bardzel, Mike Mensink, Mark Rapacz, Dawn Frederick, and Steve Norman. You all help keep me rolling through the wilderness.

Finally, the work of Laura Ingalls Wilder was a major influence on this novel, both the Little House series and *Pioneer Girl: The Annotated Autobiography*. Her talents for description and capturing the power of simple, raw emotion are extraordinary. May we all keep our eyes and hearts open to the wondrous nature of the world as well as she did.

About the Author

David is the author of 2016 MN Book Award finalist *The Firebug of Balrog County* (Flux), the Bram Stoker-nominated *The Suicide Collectors* (St. Martin's Press), *And the Hills Opened Up* (Burnt Bridge), and *Wormwood, Nevada* (St. Martin's Press). He holds an MFA in Writing from Hamline University and a BA in English from St. Olaf College. He lives in St. Paul, Minnesota.

You can visit David's website at davidoppegaard.com.